"You haven't changed, Gabby."

Her stomach plunked to her feet.

"I resent that."

"Why?"

"Why?" Since Cal had left town, she'd shaved off twenty pounds and had grown out the curly hair she used to control by keeping it shaped like a spongy football helmet around her head. Sadly she was missing a fashion chromosome, so her wardrobe had transformed only to the extent that she now bought smaller-size jeans and tucked in the blouses she wore to work. Still, she had made a true attempt this past decade and a half to look better, and it was beyond frustrating to discover that her makeover made no impression at all on someone who hadn't seen her since shortly after she'd turned in her high school cap and gown.

"No thirty-three-year-old woman wants to be told she seems the same as she did at eighteen."

Cal walked toward her. "I liked you fine at eighteen."

He kept coming until they were inches apart, and Gabby felt every nerve sizzle.

Dear Reader,

Many of the characters in the Home Sweet Honeyford series are based on my own family. You may recognize them!

My Uncle Henry had a new joke every day. From him I learned: life is hard, now go play. Henry Berns and Poppy Max of *Caleb's Bride* have a lot in common with him.

From my father I learned that some men will go the extra mile to ensure their families are safe and well cared for. Caleb Wells is like that. Committed to giving his daughter the childhood he never had, Cal moves back to Honeyford, where no dream is too broken to be put back together again.

My mother, Laura Lea, taught me that nothing has to be perfect to be beautiful—not a body, not a relationship, not a life. It's a lesson Gabby Coombs must learn before she can grab the beautiful life awaiting her with Cal and his daughter.

Enjoy your stay in Honeyford, where life is, perhaps, just a little bit sweeter!

Wendy Warren

CALEB'S BRIDE

WENDY WARREN

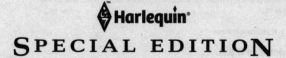

Harlequin®

SPECIAL EDITION

Recycling programs
for this product may
not exist in your area.

ISBN-13: 978-0-373-65622-6

CALEB'S BRIDE

Copyright © 2011 by Wendy Warren

Printed in U.S.A.

Recent books by Wendy Warren

Harlequin Special Edition

†*Caleb's Bride* #2140

Silhouette Special Edition

Dakota Bride #1463
Making Babies #1644
Undercover Nanny #1710
**The Boss and Miss Baxter* #1737
Once More, at Midnight #1817
**The Baby Bargain #1820
†*The Cowboy's Convenient
    Bride* #2068
†*Something Unexpected* #2105

Silhouette Romance

Mr. Wright #936
Romantics Anonymous #981
Oh, Baby! #1033
Her Very Own Husband #1148
Just Say I Do #1236
The Drifter's Gift #1268
The Oldest Virgin in Oakdale #1609

*Family Business
**Logan's Legacy Revisited
†Home Sweet Honeyford

WENDY WARREN

lives in the Pacific Northwest with her actor husband, their wonderful daughter and the assorted four-legged and finned creatures they bring home. A two-time recipient of Romance Writers of America's RITA® Award, Wendy loves to read and write the kind of books that remind her of the old movies she grew up watching with her mom and now shares with her own daughter—stories about decent people looking for the love that can make an ordinary life extraordinary. When not writing, she likes to take long walks under leafy trees, lift weights that make her sweat and her husband laugh, settle in for cozy chats with great friends, and pretend she will someday win a million dollars in a bake-off. Check out her website, www.authorwendywarren.com, for more information on Honeyford, some great recipes from the townsfolk and other fun stuff.

For Libbi
My daughter and teacher, in-house comic relief
and dream come true.
I need only to think of you to feel blessed beyond words.
"Mom" is the best name ever.

Prologue

Dear Diary,

It's official: I'm in LOVE.

Lesley and I went to the pharmacy after school to get root beer floats because it was like record degrees out and also because I wanted to see DEAN. Hideous Len, who was hanging around the soda fountain doing nothing *as usual* goes, "Maybe you should make that *diet* root beer for Flabby Gabby."

Caleb Wells was there and he hit Len so hard Len fell off the stool. Then Caleb picked him up and shouted, "Apologize, Imbecile!"

Lesley thought that was the most romantic thing ever. I thought he looked like a gladiator—his arms got really muscley this year—but Caleb Wells is like practically my brother, so it wasn't r-o-m-a-n-t-I-c.

But then DEAN…DEEEEEAAAAAAN…comes over and goes (I am quoting, he said it exactly like this), "Guys.

Let's work it out without punching, okay? Len, apologize to Gabrielle, because that was a really ignorant remark."

That was what he said (plus also he smiled at me sooo sweetly!) and that completely put Len in his place, and after he apologized Dean looked at me a reeeeaaaallly long time and said, "You look nice in pink, Gabrielle." OH. MY. GOD!!!!!!

Dean Kingsley is the most mature, most gentle, most WONDERFUL boy in this entire town, and I LOVE him. I will never love Anyone. Else.

Yours truly,

Gabby—age thirteen, which is old enough to know THIS IS NOT A CRUSH.

P.S. I am on a diet as of right NOW, but NOT because of Hideous Len. Just because I probably should be and also I want to make Dean feel proud when he's with me.

P.P.S. The fact that he is two years older than me is absolutely perfect according to Lesley, who says older men make the best lovers.

Chapter One

"Just when the caterpillar thought life was over, it became a butterfly."
—Anonymous

Twenty years later...

"You can do this." Perspiration dotted Gabrielle Coombs's forehead as she aimed her fountain pen at the papers on the desk in front of her. "You *have* to do this."

Clutching the pen so hard her knuckles turned white, Gabby forced her shaking hand toward the real-estate document that would put her business, Honey Comb's Barbershop, up for sale. Her heart quaked as much as her hand. She'd only worked in one place her entire life, and it was right here in this century-old, brick-walled storefront.

"'One cannot look into a bright future if her eyes are

filled with tears from the past,'" she quoted aloud, pressing the quivering ballpoint to the signature line, but her
fingers refused to move.

Spouting insights was easy. One of the signs in her
window read "Haircuts—$10. Wisdom—priceless." Her
grandfather Max had started the custom of sharing phil-
osophical quotes with his customers over fifty years ago.
When he'd passed Honey Comb's to Gabby, she'd gladly
picked up the torch. She must have had hundreds of quotes
packed into her brain by now. But talk was cheap unless
action backed it up. Action—that was the hard part.

"Life is like crossing a set of monkey bars. You have to
let go to move forward." She muttered one of her grandfather's favorite sayings, and taking one big deep breath,
scrawled her name.

Wide-eyed and perspiring, she looked at the page. "Oh,
my God, I'm really doing it."

Unexpectedly, a chunk of anxiety fell away like rusted
armor. Refusing to give herself time to chicken out, she
quickly penned the date then signed on the other lines the
real-estate agent had indicated.

For as long as Gabby could remember, she had planned
to do two things with her life: Run Honey Comb's—the
coziest, warmest place on earth, and marry Dean Kingsley—the coziest, warmest *man* on the planet.

"'The best laid schemes of mice and men do often go
awry...'"

Despite the fact that Dean had never been anything
other than friendly and kind, Gabby had convinced herself that he would fall for her when she was thinner, pret-
tier, funnier. When she figured out how to keep her red
hair from frizzing in the summer, or when she'd read all
his favorite books. His love was going to be the chrysalis

that changed her from plain, awkward Gabby Coombs to confident, graceful butterfly.

Dean had screwed up her great plan by falling in love with someone else. Someone who had been a stranger to all of them until only a few months ago. Now the man she'd dreamed about for twenty years (twenty—*aaaaaagh!*) was married with a child on the way, and Gabby felt like an old train that had rattled too long on the same dusty route, never veering from its chosen course but expecting the scenery magically to change.

Well, not anymore.

"It's time for me to say goodbye, Poppy." She lifted her gaze to the framed black-and-white photo of the man who had given her this barbershop on her twenty-third birthday, nearly one decade ago. Despite her firm conviction (it really was firm), tears filled her eyes. "I hope you understand."

Her benevolent grandfather smiled down at her, leaning against the striped barber pole that, to this day, swirled like a dancing peppermint stick out front.

Six weeks earlier, on a whim, Gabby had applied for a job that would take her far from her hometown of Honeyford, Oregon. Three days ago she'd received an offer of employment from Rising Sun Cruises. The next morning she'd accepted the offer, and yesterday she had visited the real-estate agent to put her business up for sale.

Bold moves, every one, which was exactly what she needed right now. Bold moves to create a brand new life.

And a brand new Gabby.

When a knock rattled the barbershop's glass door, she realized she was several minutes past opening, something she couldn't recall ever happening before. Jumping from her stool behind the small front desk, she headed for the door.

Wiping the moisture from beneath her eyes, she smoothed a hand over the kinky hair that inevitably escaped her ponytail and turned the key in the lock. She plastered a smile on her face as she swung the door open, but words of welcome died on her lips. Surprise—and the stirrings of something that felt like dread—tensed every muscle.

June sunshine silhouetted a tall man with square shoulders. As Gabby's eyes adjusted to the light, she saw that he was gorgeous—*still* gorgeous—in a way few males in Honeyford were. An edgy, mysterious, dangerous kind of gorgeous.

"Hi, there. Can I get a haircut?"

The lump of emotion filling Gabby's throat all morning doubled at the sound of his voice, which was deeper, more gravelly than it had been fifteen years earlier when Caleb Wells had been an eighteen-year-old farmhand bound and determined to make something of himself.

Her gaze rose to his chestnut hair. Thick, wavy and glittering with deep bronze-and-gold highlights, it had obviously been expertly styled.

"You don't need a haircut," she said, her voice hoarse with shock. "You look…" She hesitated.

As a teen, Cal had been whipcord lean, perpetually hungry looking. Now in his thirties, he impressively filled his designer suit. As sharp as three points of a triangle, the chin and jaw that used to sport a light shadow were smooth and whisker-free.

"You look good," she concluded, feeling her face flame.

The right side of his mouth curled just a bit in response.

He turned his head, glancing into the barbershop. "May I come in?"

Gabby hesitated, apprehension tingling throughout her body.

One of the signs in her window warned, "No Shoes, No Shirt, You Better Get Your Hair Cut Someplace Else," but Cal looked more like the CEO of a Fortune 1000 company than a small-town kid who'd once struggled by on odd jobs and church handouts. Since she couldn't justify keeping him out, Gabby stepped back and got a whiff of expensive cologne as Cal brushed past her. Whatever he'd been doing all these years, he'd managed to effect a complete transformation.

How ironic, she thought dazedly, feeling as if she were having an out-of-body experience, *that Cal Wells, of all people, should reappear again now, when I'm about to take the biggest risk of my life.*

A decade and a half ago, *he* had been the biggest risk she'd ever taken. And that time she had concluded she'd made an awful mistake.

As Cal entered the barbershop, his gaze moved to the wall of black-and-white pictures that framed the large mirrors above Honey Comb's two cutting stations. The photos, most of which she'd taken, were the only things that changed in the shop on a regular basis.

While Cal moved closer, studying her work, Gabby busied herself opening the blinds and flipping the sign that said, "Shut Till We're Not," to the side that announced, "Come In Already."

Several times she glanced over her shoulder, until Cal caught her gaze in the mirror and raised a brow.

"Your photos?" he asked, indicating the display.

She nodded.

Again he gave her that flicker of a smile. "You're good. I knew you would be."

Her heart stuttered a little in response. "Thanks." How many times had she taken photos of him while he'd worked on her family's farm? Hidden from view, she'd snapped candid shots, using the rough and beautiful Oregon land-scape as the perfect backdrop for Cal's untamed looks and solitary personality. Her family had praised the many photos she took of them all, but only Cal had truly studied her work, commenting on the light and the composition. Telling her that her work showed "passion."

"So how about that haircut?"

Slowly she shook her head. "You don't need it."

Still looking at her in the mirror, he ran a hand over the thick waves. "I do. It's too long."

Because his hair was trimmed neatly above his ears, the comment surprised her. "It's shorter than I've ever seen it. It was way past your shoulders the last time—" With the nature of their last encounter—and its aftermath—filling her mind, Gabby fumbled. "—the last time I saw you."

Cal turned toward her, pinning her with the unwavering hazel gaze that had always hidden more than it revealed. "I haven't tried to wear my hair like a rock star for years, Gabrielle. It's time for a trim. And you were always the best." When she continued to stare without speaking, he pressed, "It wouldn't make you uncomfortable, would it? Now that I think about it, cutting my hair used to make you pretty damn nervous."

"No, it didn't." Automatic and defensive, her denial made Cal grin.

A real grin, not the partial, inscrutable smile charac-teristic of him. This one was full and beautiful, which was strange since the boy Gabby had known came from a home life that hadn't offered up many reasons to smile. She felt slightly woozy now, trying to remember when she'd last seen unreserved enjoyment on his face. Then he said, "You haven't changed, Gabby," and her stomach plunked to her feet.

"I resent that."

The brow arched higher. "Why?"

"Why?" Because fifteen years ago she had looked like little Orphan Annie on steroids, and he damn well knew it!

Since Cal had left town, she'd shaved off twenty pounds and had grown out the curly hair she used to control by keeping it shaped like a spongy football helmet around her head. Sadly, she was missing a fashion chromosome, so her wardrobe had transformed only to the extent that she now bought smaller size jeans and tucked in the blouses she wore to work. Still, she had made a true attempt this past decade and a half to look better, and it was beyond frustrating to discover that her makeover made no impression at all on someone who hadn't seen her since shortly after she'd turned in her high school cap and gown.

In an effort to preserve some dignity, she kept her tone instructional rather than plaintive. "No thirty-three-year-old woman wants to be told she seems the same as she did at eighteen."

Cal walked toward her. "I liked you fine at eighteen."

He kept coming until they were inches apart, and Gabby felt every nerve sizzle.

"Remember the first time you cut my hair?" he asked, his voice softer than it needed to be given that there was no one else in the shop to overhear them. "You'd been practicing on your brothers. You made them sit through three haircuts each before you agreed to work on me. And then you only did it because they took off like rockets the second they saw you coming."

"Well," she said, wanting like crazy to back up a couple of steps, but refusing to divulge how nervous he really did make her. "I thought I should practice on family first."

Though she hadn't thought of it in ages, the day he mentioned popped vividly to mind. She could picture the way he'd leaned against her mother's kitchen counter, drinking lemonade and eating shortbread while her brothers squirmed and complained about the dishtowels around their necks and their fear that Gabby might scalp them. Having just turned fifteen, but seeming years older, Cal had stood silently, observing, until finally she'd run out of siblings. Then he'd pushed away from the counter and announced, "My turn."

Now those strange, translucent eyes of his narrowed slightly, and she realized she might have hurt his feelings by suggesting he wasn't "family." Throughout his teens, he'd practically lived at the Coombses' farm, hanging out with her brothers and being as helpful to her parents as one of their own children. Maybe more. Her mother had lived to feed him, because unlike her own sometimes picky kids, Cal had always eaten two helpings of everything.

Only Cal and Gabby had never quite bridged the gap between friend and family.

"We're not kids anymore," he said. "I think we can both handle a haircut. Don't you?"

Challenge filled his expression.

No. Absolutely not. I am a sissy.

"Of course."

Cal's eyes flickered with what Gabby suspected was amusement. Swallowing the last of her reticence, she nodded toward one of the two old-fashioned barber chairs. "Have a seat. You'll probably want to take off that fancy suit jacket, though. You can hang it on the coat tree by the front desk. I've got to go in back to get a cape."

He nodded. "Sounds good."

Leaving him, Gabby headed to the rear of the shop and the laundry bag she'd brought with her this morning. Extracting a clean stack of neatly folded capes and a pile of white washcloths, she moved with the sureness of someone who had performed this task literally thousands of times. Inside, however, she felt like grape jelly.

How could she casually cut his hair after what had happened the last time they were together?

Detouring into a small restroom with a single overhead lightbulb, Gabby yanked the cord that illuminated the room.

She winced as she peered into the mirror. The red curls she typically bundled into a ponytail at the nape of her neck looked like a nuclear blast in Technicolor. Escaped tendrils provided fallout all around her head.

Setting aside the capes and towels, she quickly reassembled the 'do, scraping her feral hair into something more managed. She didn't need to look attractive for him. But she would like to exude confidence and self-possession, two qualities that had been in short supply fifteen years ago. Digging a tube of lip balm from her front pocket, she swiped it over her dry lips.

There was a whole river of white water under the bridges she and Cal had burned, and frankly she hated to churn it up, especially now. On the brink of personal change, she wanted to feel confident and bold—not to be reminded of one of the most awkward moments in her entire life.

It's been fifteen years, Gabby.

To Cal, what had happened the last summer after their senior year in high school was probably nothing more than a dim recollection. Maybe an anecdote. He was a guy, after all. He'd walked away from Honeyford, from her family and from his best friends that year. One sexually inexperienced young woman desperate to discover what she was missing in life was unlikely to hold a place in his long-term memory.

The fact was that with a father, three brothers and a

grandpa who owned a barbershop, Gabby had considered herself fairly comfortable around men (the ones she wasn't hoping to marry). But Cal Wells, with his silent stares and inscrutable expressions, had always been the exception. Cal had thrown her off-kilter and…that one evening, anyway…excited her.

Hardening her gray eyes at the mirror, she made her reflection a solemn promise. "That was then, this is now. The old Gabby may have been a fuzzy caterpillar, but the new and improved Gabrielle Coombs is a butterfly, graceful and free.

"If he can act as if nothing happened, so can you." Gabby gave herself a smile. Shoulders back, chin high, she collected her capes and towels and returned to the front of the shop.

Cal stood a couple of feet from her front desk, his suit jacket off, his hands in his trouser pockets. A sober, contemplative expression furrowed his brow as he studied a photo of her grandfather.

"He always liked you," Gabby offered, knowing it was true. Max had considered Caleb Wells an old soul. "He said you had integrity."

Slowly, Cal turned his head. Something that looked like pain flashed through his eyes. "I liked him, too."

Crossing to the leather-cushioned barber chair, Gabby waited for Cal to follow. His serious expression was beginning to border on grim. The thoughts that hid behind his eyes seemed particularly alive and active now, even more so than when he'd first walked through the door.

For a moment she wondered if he'd changed his mind about the haircut, but then he moved, seating himself and patiently allowing her to adjust a paper collar and white towel around the neck of his dress shirt.

In their senior year of high school, Gabby's best friend,

Lesley, who had started dating her oldest brother, Eric, by that time, had claimed that Cal possessed "mystique." Also, that he had lips made for kissing. Gabby, who, tragically, had yet to experience her first kiss at that point, could only wonder.

Lesley should see his lips now.

Matured, Cal's features looked as if a master sculptor had carved them in a burst of love for the human race. His lips had clearly defined peaks, their fullness perfect for photographing and…other things. Lesley had married Eric shortly after college, eventually providing two adorable nieces for Gabby to spoil, but she was still willing to discuss a man's kissing potential…for Gabby's sake.

Best friends, sisters-in-law and confidants, she and Les had shared a lot of info with each other over the years, but not even Lesley knew that the kissing potential of Cal's lips was no longer a mystery to Gabby.

"Something wrong?"

"Huh?" she answered stupidly, jerking to attention and watching the very lips she was pondering rise slightly— right side only, as usual.

His translucent eyes narrowed. "You seem…ruffled, Gabby. Something bothering you?"

"No. I'm not ruffled. Just deciding what to do with your hair. How much do you want off?"

"Enough so that I won't need another trim for at least a month. I'm heading into a busy time. Afraid I may not get to a barber again for a while."

"Okay." Flipping open a cape, she settled it around him. *Treat him like any other client.* "So, Cal, what brings you back to—"

"How've you been, Gabby?"

They spoke over each other.

Clipping the ends of the cape together, Gabby reached

for a comb and spray bottle of water and forced herself to smile. "Me first."

"All right."

"What brings you back to Honeyford? No, no, wait. First why don't you tell me where you've been all these years?"

"Chicago," he answered, accommodating her. "I went to the University of Illinois for graduate school, got an internship position in my field then stayed on with the company."

Gabby spritzed his hair. "Graduate school." She was impressed. Glad for him, too, because she understood the significance of his earning a master's degree. No one else in his family had completed high school. Alcoholism had taken its toll on his relatives, diminishing their ability to work or parent in anything more than spurts of sobriety. Cal had spent most of his teen years trying to establish a clear difference between himself and the rest of the Wells clan, and it looked as if he'd accomplished his goal. "What's your field?"

"Environmental engineering."

Okay, she was *really* impressed. "Sounds like a good fit. You always loved the outdoors."

Cal shrugged his broad shoulders. "I got a great job offer. The kind a kid who never had two nickels to rub together couldn't pass up. As for being a good fit, I worked in a high rise, as a corporate consultant."

Which explained the expensive suit, she supposed.

Setting the spray bottle down, she picked up her comb and scissors. Lifting the first hank of hair she planned to snip, feeling the thick silkiness, her fingers buzzed with the sudden, unexpected memory of the last time she had touched his hair.

Back then, her touch had been tentative, her fingers

clumsy. Definitely more fuzzy worm than graceful butterfly. When *he'd* touched *her,* however, there had been an undeniable moment of exhilarating flight....

"So—" she cleared her throat, trying to change the channel in her mind "—you said, 'worked.' Past tense?"

"Very past tense."

Forcing herself to focus on the actions that gave her confidence, Gabby took the first cut. *Keep talking. Talking relaxes the client...and the barber.* "You're changing fields, then?"

As she began to work in earnest, snips of shiny brown hair floated to the cape like confetti. "Positions," he responded. "I found a job that pays less, but I'll be working *on* the land."

"Where will you be—"

"Nope."

"What?"

He looked up through the hair she'd pushed over his forehead. "How long have I known you?"

Gabby blinked at the unexpected question. "Well, technically we haven't seen each other for—"

"Forget 'technically.'" His gaze toughened. "Here are the stats. Years we've known each other—twenty. Times you've allowed conversations deeper than a puddle—fewer than a handful. Why is that, Gabby? I never noticed you skirting meaningful conversations with anyone else."

Gabby faltered, blindsided, and loathing the feeling of being transparent. Yes, she had avoided deeper conversations with Cal. She'd put on a pretty good front with others, but Cal had read her too easily for her own comfort.

Sending her scissors skimming across the ends of his hair, she murmured, "I'm happy to have a conversation on any topic you like, but I want to finish your trim before my morning rush starts, so—"

"Let's start with the topic of this barbershop," he interrupted. "Why you're selling it, for example. And whether it has anything at all to do with Dean Kingsley."

Chapter Two

The scissors slipped, knicking Gabby's knuckle. "Damn," she swore, shaking the pained hand. After checking for blood (hardly any), she gaped at Cal in the mirror. "How do you know I'm—"

The answer came to her before she completed the sentence. She glanced toward the coat tree, where she'd told him to hang his jacket, then to the desk sitting right beside it, and her gape turned into a glare. "You snooped around my desk? When I went in the back? You read my private papers!"

"I glanced over," he admitted. "Your 'private papers' are sitting out where anyone can see them, Gabrielle."

"Anyone who leans over to read the fine print," she snapped. Leaving him, she rushed to the desk to conceal the real-estate document. Good gravy, she didn't need any of her other customers to walk in, read the papers and realize she was selling the shop—before she broke the news to her own family! Shoving the papers into a drawer, she slammed it shut…along with the scissors and comb she'd brought with her. Realizing her mistake, she yanked the drawer open, pulled out her tools and rounded on Caleb. "You couldn't have known what those papers were about at a glance. You were snooping."

As cool as ever, he shrugged. "I spent the morning at Honeyford Realty. I recognized their paperwork. Are you selling because of Kingsley?"

Resentment, hot and humid, filled Gabby from the stomach up.

Even though she'd tried to keep her infatuation for Dean under wraps, she knew Cal had figured out her secret.

Now his supernatural eyes pinned her to the spot. He looked like a boa constrictor laughing at a mouse.

"News still travels fast in Honeyford," he said. "I bet I wasn't downtown more than an hour before I heard that Kingsley got married a couple of months ago." Cal's head tsk-tsked slowly from side to side. "You're not just selling the shop, are you? You're running away."

"Beep, beep! Comin' through!"

Before Gabby could respond to Cal, Henry Berns, owner of Honey Bea's Bakery across the street, opened the barbershop door. Pressing one scrawny shoulder against the glass, he bustled over the threshold, his knobby hands occupied with a pink pastry box. "Gotta set this down before I drop it. Don't have the muscle strength I used to."

Gabby watched Henry as if she were standing outside herself, a tight band of emotion constricting her breath so that she felt incapable of heaving a single word into her mouth.

Nearly a foot shorter than Cal, Henry nodded at the much younger man, whom he gave no indication of recognizing, then placed the string-wrapped box on the desk and winked at Gabby. "It's a Dobish Torte. Two pounds of dark chocolate for my best girl." Toddling happily to the vacant chair, he told Gabby, "You go ahead and finish up. I'll grab a seat before the morning rush." With a spryness that belied his seventy-five years (and the claim that he lacked muscle strength), Henry hopped into the chair next to Cal's, helped himself to a comb and worked it through the gray waves he kept stiffly pomaded.

By sheer force of will, Gabby managed to murmur her thanks for the cake.

"Why, sure. Sweets for my sweetheart!" The old man winked into the mirror.

A knowing smile spread across Cal's face, and Gabby blushed.

All her life she had felt a little more awkward, a little less beautiful than the girls around her, which was probably why the thought of Dean Kingsley had filled her with such joy. Dean had seemed so golden, so rich with gentlemanly grace, an innate country suave that had afforded Gabby countless hours of pleasure fantasizing about becoming Mrs. Country Suave.

In the barber chair to Cal's right, Henry Berns hummed happily while perusing the latest copy of *The Honeyford Buzz.* All her most serious suitors were over seventy. Nothing had changed, and Cal knew it. As the curve of his lips bloomed into a full grin, Gabby felt once again that uncomfortable, haunting sense of déjà vu.

Reaching into his back pocket, Cal withdrew an expensive-looking leather wallet as he crossed toward her. Withdrawing a bill for the trim she hadn't completed, he laid it on her desk. "See you around, Gabrielle."

The door clicked softly shut behind him, and suddenly Gabby remembered exactly when she'd last seen

his grin—full of enjoyment and humor and mischief—
prior to today.

It had happened fourteen years, ten months and three
weeks ago. The summer they'd graduated from high
school.

Dean had come home from college to work in his father's pharmacy, and Gabby had decided the time had
come: She was going to tell her beloved exactly how she
felt so they could begin their life together. Her courage
stoked, her expectations huge and glorious, she waited for
Dean to arrive at the Fourth of July celebration downtown.
But when he showed up, there was a girl clinging happily
to his arm, a lovely girl he introduced to everyone as the
woman he hoped to marry.

Numb at first, feeling frozen inside, Gabby somehow
managed to smile and congratulate Dean along with everyone else. Two hours past the fireworks display, however, her emotions thawed and the misery poured out in
waves so overpowering it was difficult to breathe.

She had expected to become a woman in Dean's arms.
The best moments of her life were supposed to have happened with him. At eighteen, she had yet to experience
her first kiss. Suddenly, it all seemed like such a horrid
waste.

That was when Gabrielle Coombs decided enough was
enough and threw herself at a boy for the very first time.

And Cal Wells took pity and made love to her.

Cal slipped on a pair of ridiculously expensive sunglasses, a gift from his ex-wife, who had never met a label
she didn't like. The dark glasses gave him the comforting
illusion of privacy. He preferred not to make eye contact
with others this morning. Not that many people in town
were likely to remember him or would rush to welcome

him back even if they did, but Cal's emotions were running so high at the moment that he didn't want to make small talk.

Gabrielle Coombs. She was still here, in their hometown. Still single from what he gathered. And, even though she hadn't admitted a thing, he'd bet his last paycheck that she was still in love with Dean Kingsley.

Beneath his breath, Cal muttered a word that would cost his ten-year-old daughter a dollar if she said it.

"I acted like a jackass." He spoke out loud to himself, a habit he'd gotten into since his marriage disintegrated. He'd gone years during which his lengthiest adult conversations occurred as he looked into the mirror while he was shaving. "Gabby never got over him," he muttered.

Fifteen years ago, when Cal headed back to college after what had amounted to the best and worst summer of his life, he'd assumed that if he ever returned to Honeyford, he'd find Gabby married with kids, a home, a PTA membership. Her husband, he figured, would love her, but would have no clue as to how lucky he was to be part of the Coombs clan.

Cal would have known.

For five years—from the time he was thirteen until he'd gone off to college—Cal had spent every minute he could on the Coombses' farm, making himself too useful for anyone to complain about his constant presence, studying every detail of normal family life as if there'd be a pop quiz at the end of each week.

He'd met two of Gabby's brothers in wood shop at school, and they'd invited him home one afternoon to hang out. Their mother, Nancy, had made an enormous platter of sandwiches *as a snack*—not even for dinner, which had astounded him. At that time in his life, he was lucky to scrounge up enough food for a single daily meal at home. Nancy had insisted they all wash their hands before they touched a bite. While her sons had rolled their eyes and protested, their perpetually smiling mother had kept up a running commentary about the baseball jerseys she had mended that day, the old clothes she'd boxed and wanted her sons to drop off at the church, and the barn dance she would like them to attend, because "Lord knows your wives will thank me someday." Cal had listened to the woman's every word and followed her instructions without a peep.

For years he had wondered whether such a family existed outside of television reruns. After he'd found them, and even though they hadn't belonged to him, he had known instantly that he wanted to be asked back again and again. And he had been. To this day, he counted what he had learned in the Coombses' old farmhouse to be one of his greatest blessings.

Maybe you wanted Gabby so you could become a permanent part of the family. Maybe that's all it ever was.

The old explanation, the one he'd been running through his head for years, cropped up again, and as always he played with it awhile, half-hoping he could make it ring true.

The thing was, that very first day on the farm he realized Gabby was someone special. His first clue had been when she'd admitted to her father, Frank, that she'd hidden one of their older lambs, Chester, until she could "talk some sense into" Frank and make him see that the little guy should be a pet, not a lamb chop. She spoke with persuasive passion and loyalty, claiming that vegetarianism would be better for the whole family. A few weeks later she saved a spider from the shoe her brother Ben had been about to hammer it with, and more times than Cal could count, Gabby showered the people in her sphere with a similar protectiveness. In school she befriended the new, the awkward and the adrift, pulling them into her circle of friends. She wasn't one of the most popular girls, but she was well-liked.

Despite the fact that she'd never shown him quite the same level of concern, Cal felt drawn to the sensitive girl. He enjoyed feeling like one of her brothers and reminded himself that he didn't want anyone treating him like some defenseless lamb or brainless bug, anyway, so who cared if sometimes she kept her distance? By the time he turned fifteen, however, he knew he was nursing a crush on Gabby. She represented something innocent and good. Something he wanted in his own life. Something that could change him.

At seventeen, he'd realized he didn't stand a chance with her. In a million years he wouldn't be able to measure up to the golden boy Dean Kingsley, whom Gabby appeared to love with a loyalty Cal would happily die to feel…from someone.

At eighteen, Cal graduated from high school, the first person in his family of drug addicts and wastrels to do so, and he graduated on the honor roll. He had a college scholarship, a student loan, a dorm room waiting for him and more self-esteem than ever in his life. And he still thought about Gabby.

So, when he found her crying in the gazebo in Doc Kingsley park after the July Fourth fireworks display, her spirit crushed because Dean had returned from college for the summer with a girlfriend on his arm, Cal claimed that exquisitely vulnerable moment for himself and became Gabby Coombs's first lover. He and Gabby had been two young people hungry to be held.

It had been an aching, tender, heartbreaking night…

each of them wanting someone who didn't return the feelings.

Cal's steps slowed as he realized he was abreast of King's Pharmacy, the business Dean's father had owned. Dean had worked here through high school. And Gabby had gone in on one fabricated excuse or another every chance she'd gotten.

Turning toward the window with its large gold lettering, Cal noted the sign that read, *Dean Kingsley, Pharmacist on Duty.* The golden boy had not disappointed. Cal shook his head. "You could have had her if you'd crooked your finger."

In the morning sun, Cal studied his reflection in the glass. Well-groomed, well-dressed and, when he wasn't acting like a petulant imbecile, well-spoken; he was a far cry from the boy he'd been. Back then, he'd been a struggling youth with a messy past, and he doubted that anyone, including Gabby's parents and brothers, would have preferred him over Dean Kingsley as her boyfriend. Against the bright light of the doctor's perfect son, Cal hadn't been able to shine at all.

Turning away from the pharmacy, Cal strode up the street. Some of the best advice he'd ever gotten had come from Gabby's own grandfather. Max was the only person Cal had ever told about his confusing feelings for Gabrielle. He'd even considered turning down his scholarship so he could remain in Honeyford, near her.

Begged for a clue about how to claim Gabby's attention, Max had put a hand on Cal's shoulder. "Son, if you keep one foot in the past and one in the future, you're going to piss all over today. Just keep moving."

Sound advice. There had been more, but that was the plainspoken guidance Cal had followed.

He planned to follow it again now.

His heart both hardened and softened as he thought of Minna, his beautiful, smart, talented, anxious daughter, who, so far, had been as unlucky in love as Cal. He had returned to Honeyford to give Minna the family they hadn't been able to build in Chicago. The Coombs clan was the example he wanted to emulate.

He couldn't afford another episode like today's. He'd been rude and insinuating to the Coombses' only daughter, a woman with whom he'd had no contact in fifteen years. What business was it of his whether she was staying, going or planning a trip to the moon?

Cal would die for his daughter. With a failed marriage to her mother, and no role models among his own relations, he required the Coombses' guidance on how to create a successful, stable family.

If that meant killing off the last vestiges of his fantasies about Gabby, so be it.

By eight-thirty on Friday evening, only five hardy souls remained at the Honeyford Days Fourth of July Celebration Committee meeting. Unseasonably sultry June weather and Vernon Reynaud's refusal to contribute to "wasteful government spending" by turning on the air-conditioning in the community center had considerably thinned their ranks. Gabby and Lesley remained, however, Lesley doodling idly on a yellow legal pad, and Gabby eyeballing the Honey Bunz—puffy croissant-style pastry balls with a crunchy honey coating—donated for the committee's sustenance by Honey Bea's bakery.

"No, leave it. We're having dessert later," Lesley whispered as Gabby's fingers snaked toward a Honey Bunz.

"Right. Thanks." She snatched her hand back, but holy sugar rush, Batman, did she long for the distraction of a quality insulin surge. She'd been horribly depressed since this morning.

"How late can you stay out tonight?" she whispered to her sis-in-law.

"Probably until ten," Les whispered back. "I warned Eric I'd be late. He's at your parents' with the girls. What's the matter with you? You keep kicking the table leg."

"Are we still discussing the plans for Honeyford Days or have we decided to adjourn?" Flo Bixby raised her rickety voice above the irresponsible extraneous chatter in the room.

"Adjourn, I beg you," Lesley muttered under her breath, but she rallied for the cause, smiling nicely at Flo and offering a succinct update on her choreography for Honeyford, A Retrospective in Dance, being presented by the Dancing Honeybees Senior Tappers.

As the secretary for tonight's meeting, Gabby dutifully took notes, but her mind was a million miles away. She had a plan for The Radical Improvement of Gabrielle Coombs, a plan she intended to begin instituting immediately, and, forgive her, but plotting her transformation trumped working on yet another Independence Day lollapalooza. After this morning, she'd like to ignore July Fourth and its loaded memories altogether.

Cal's reappearance and his pointed comments had whipped up a tumultuous sea of self-recriminations inside her. She'd been pretty successful over the years at burying the memory of the July Fourth when she'd lost her virginity to Cal Wells, but after his visit to Honey Comb's, images from that long-ago night had been forming in her mind, growing sharper and clearer all day.

She recalled vividly, for example, that he'd found her in the dark shelter of the Doc Kingsley Park gazebo, sitting all alone, yielding to pitiful tears that had poured down her cheeks and trickled like brine into her mouth. The brackish flavor only partially masked the bitterness of Dean's announcement that he was serious about the lithe beauty he'd brought home from college, someone he had known less than a year.

Gabby had spent five times that long trying to make Dean see her as a romantic possibility.

When the July Fourth fireworks had died down and most everyone filed out of the park, Gabby curled up on the gazebo bench and gave in to silent sobs that stabbed her abdomen. Time seemed irrelevant at that point, but she didn't think she'd been there too long when a voice reached her, so soft and close that she jumped.

"Don't cry."

She'd turned to see Cal climbing the gazebo steps, his angular features tense in the moonlight. His plea, pained and earnest, only made her cry harder, however, and after a moment he'd slid onto the bench beside her. "Damn it, Gabby, don't…"

She'd felt his strong arm curl around her shoulders, the unexpectedness of the gesture temporarily interrupting the flow of her tears. Other than the times when she cut his hair or he helped her with chores around the farm, they didn't touch.

Through the shadows in the gazebo, she'd looked at him, her heart breaking, lips wobbling.

"What can I do?" he'd whispered.

A tsunami of hurt and frustration and regret and need had tossed her heart around like a piece of driftwood. Wetly, she'd blinked then pleaded with no forethought whatsoever, "Kiss me…"

"Stop kicking the table." Lesley shoved an elbow into Gabby's ribs.

"Sorry." Heat flooding her cheeks, Gabby looked down

at the notes she was supposed to be taking. Some secrets were too big to tell even your very best friend.

It took another half hour for the meeting to wrap up and then Gabby grabbed Lesley's arm, hustling her to the diner, where they grabbed their favorite booth in the back and gave their order to Opal, who was hard of hearing and generally handed her ticket book to regular customers so they could write their own orders. She soon returned with a pot of decaf, a slab of marionberry pie and two forks.

"Oh, Mama, that's good," Lesley purred in appreciation.

Gabby picked up her fork. "You haven't even tasted it yet."

"I'm not talking about the pie, innocent child." Lesley nodded pointedly toward the counter, where a lone man sat, his large hands cupped around a mug of coffee.

Gabby squinted. "Isn't that the new pastor at Honeyford Presbyterian?"

"Yessiree. Pastor Keith. *Single* Pastor Keith."

"Keith doesn't sound like a pastor's name," Gabby commented, apropos of nothing, but grateful to have a moment before she launched into her own topic. Stabbing a few marionberries and a piece of crust, she moaned at the deliciousness.

"He doesn't look like a pastor, either," Lesley mused. "He looks like he should be on a TV show called *Sex In The Small Town*. Or *Desperate Worshippers*." She waggled her brows.

Gabby put a hand over her mouth to trap the berries that nearly spilled out. "You're ogling a man of the cloth? I'm telling Eric."

"I'm not ogling him for me, you ninny." Lifting her fork, she jabbed the tines at Gabby.

Gabby leaned forward, whispering fiercely. "You think

I should date the minister of Honeyford Pres? Are you kidding? I grew up in that church. If we ever got serious, I'd picture half the choir in our bedroom, singing 'Amazing Grace.'"

"Or 'Glory Hallelujah.'"

"Lesley!" Gabby shook her head at her irreverent sister-in-law.

"He's not a priest, Gabs. He can have sex. And FYI, so can you." Abandoning the fork, she snatched a few tiny containers of creamer and laced her coffee, eyeing Gabby with barely concealed impatience. "So what about it?"

"No! I told you—"

Lesley waved a hand. "Forget the gorgeous man of God." She took a fortifying sip of decaf. "I mean sex. What's your excuse for not having any?"

Gabby squirmed, ironically feeling as if her best friend had caught her *in* the act, not out of it. "How do you know I'm not having any?"

Lesley slapped the table as if she'd heard a good joke. "Please."

Gabby's glance skittered away, a mouse hoping the cat one foot away might not notice her.

"I love you, Gabs," Lesley said, sighing. "You know I'd never say anything to hurt you, but we've reached critical mass. I didn't say anything while there was still a chance that Dean might…"

"I know, I know." Plopping her elbows on the table, Gabby covered her eyes with her hands then peeked around to make sure no one they knew was nearby, but Les would not have spoken if there had been. Gabby knew her sister-in-law truly did have her best interests at heart. "If it comforts you any, I've been thinking the same thing. I'm in a rut I have to get out of. And I am. I have a plan.

But first, I need to tell you something. I need to tell *some-one*..."

Save for a brief hiatus when the waitress came by to refill their coffee cups, Gabby did not stop talking until she'd filled Lesley in on That Night with Cal. Lesley's eyes grew wider and wider, until she practically shouted, "You and Caleb?! And you never told me? I'm going to go home and write in my journal that we are nothing like Oprah and Gayle after all. But first—" She climbed so far over the table, her bosom was nearly in the pie. "How was it?"

Picking up Lesley's discarded creamer containers and stacking them, Gabby shrugged. "It was...you know...I don't know."

"You don't know? What, it was too long ago? You can't remember?"

She remembered. Sex with Cal had been desperate, frantic...

Out of control—that's what it had been. What *she* had been that night. The experience stood, in fact, as the one out-of-control moment in Gabby's highly controlled life. And her body had reveled in it, sweeping her mind right along with it.

At first, anyway.

Being a virgin at the time, she'd felt pain that had eventually allowed reality to intrude into the moment of madness, and once that happened... She shuddered. Regret and embarrassment had snuffed out lust. For her, at least. And, really, such a wild, out-of-control feeling—not her at all.

To Lesley, she responded, "I was young. And it was my first time, so...you know."

"Oh." Lesley nodded. "Right. Not great, then. My first

time with Eric left a lot to be desired, too. But we tried again the next day, and that—"

"Too much info, too much info!" Gabby covered her ears, unwilling to hear details about her eldest brother's love life.

"All right. Tell me what happened afterward for you two."

"Nothing happened. He was going away to college."

"Which left two months between the Fourth of July and September. So...?"

"So nothing. He dropped by the next day to check on me..." Reluctant to relive the details of *that* torturously awkward encounter, Gabby shook her head. "It was only a one-night thing."

Lesley made a face. "Teenage boys and sex. Gotcha."

Gabby shrugged noncommittally.

"Well, what do you want to do about it now?" Lesley questioned, finally digging into the pie that was unlikely to do any damage at all to her willowy, five-foot-nine-inch dancer's body. "You say he's back in town. I wonder how long he's staying. Maybe you two could have a do-over and get it right this time."

"No!" Gabby looked around a tad wildly, though no one new had entered the diner, and Pastor Sex Appeal was paying his bill. "Shhh. Don't even suggest that," she hissed across the table. "I'm hoping I don't run into Cal again *at all*. I want a brand new start to my life, Les. Nothing I've done up to now requires a trip down Memory Lane."

"That makes sense, I suppose." Thoughtfully, Lesley licked berry juice off her fork. "You've had *good* sex since Cal, though, right?"

Lowering her gaze, Gabby confessed, poking at a piece of pie crust.

Lesley reached for her coffee cup, narrowing her gaze

at Gabby over the rim. "I know you don't like to talk about your sex life, and I've always tried to respect that, but there has been *someone,* right?" She nodded hopefully. "Someone who made your toes curl?"

Gabby's brow knitted. She bit her lip. "Umm…no actual toe curling to report."

"Huh." Taking a sip of coffee, Lesley shrugged philosophically. "Okay. So someone who maybe wasn't the *greatest* lover, but still…?"

"Ahh, let's see…" Knuckles to her lips, Gabby closed one eye, pretending to have to think about it. "Mmmm…" She shook her head—a tiny, reluctant movement. "No."

Lesley watched her for a protracted moment, her expression a symphony of shock, horror and awe. "Gabrielle Coombs! You are not telling me that you haven't… Since that one time?"

Mouth open, Lesley braced her hands against the booth. "Are you serious? Caleb Wells has been your one and only lover?" She raised a hand to her heart. "I like a surprise as much as the next person, but this kind of shock could kill a girl!"

Chapter Three

Gabby looked frantically around the coffee shop then back to her sister-in-law. "Shhhh! You see? This is why I don't like to talk about it. It sounds worse out loud than it really is."

"No, it doesn't." Lesley was so frozen in shock, it took her a moment to move her lips again. "Gabby, you're thirty-three. Out loud or not—"

"I know!" Groaning, Gabby lowered her forehead to the table, rolling her brow slowly back and forth on the cold wood. "I know."

"How did this happen? Haven't you wanted to?"

"Of course I wanted to. But with someone I loved. And I kept, I don't know, thinking it was going to happen with Dean, and I didn't want to be…unavailable." She raised her head. "I get props for trying to hold out for true love, right?"

"You're thirty-three, not in the novitiate and practically a virgin again. No, you get no props." Lesley wagged her head. Her voice fell to a hushed tone generally reserved for announcements that all heroic attempts to resuscitate have failed. "This is bad."

Sitting up, pressing against the hard-backed booth, Gabby rubbed her sweaty palms on the rough denim covering her thighs. "Remember how in love Poppy and Grammy Joan were? How they'd look at each other, and you could tell they knew exactly what the other person was thinking?"

Lesley nodded. "Yeah. I'd catch Max staring at her picture after she died. Sometimes he'd wink at her like he thought she could see him."

"Right. They were practically a local legend. The couple nothing on this earth could part. Well, that's what I was waiting for—a forever love. Time got away from me, that's all."

The women were silent awhile. Lesley reached for her friend's hand. "Madly in love or not, you've got to start your romantic life, Gabby. The meter's running."

Sitting straighter, Gabby nodded. "That's exactly what I'm planning, Les—to start my life, romantic and otherwise." Pulling a manila envelope from the pink-and-black nylon backpack she'd brought with her, she extracted a brochure and some boldly printed trifolds, which she spread out on the table. "Look at this."

Lesley scanned the papers. "These are brochures for that new cruise line—the one that caters to singles. I read about it in *Via*." Looking up so suddenly she almost gave herself whiplash, she gasped. "Shut. Up. You're going to have meaningless cruise sex! Have you booked the trip?"

"No, no. I'm not going on a trip. I'm going to work, Les. On the ship."

Lesley blinked. "Work. Wha— Where?" She stabbed

a finger at the brochure. "On one of these floating bedrooms?"

"It's not a floating bedroom. They're not like that. Singles' cruises are—" Gabby tried to remember how the brochure had put it "—a way to experience exciting destinations with a sophisticated group of like-minded adventurers." She smiled.

"And then have sex with them?"

"Lesley." Directing her in-law's attention to the color photograph, she said, "Look, they have waterslide races."

"Ahh, yes. The sophisticated waterslide race." Lesley shook her head slowly. "Gab, I don't get it. You're going to apply to this cruise line, and if they hire you...do what with the barbershop?"

"I already applied," Gabby corrected, gauging her sister-in-law's reaction and realizing that Lesley, who should be the easiest sell of all the Coombs, was nonetheless struggling with the news. "They *did* hire me. I'm going to be the ship's barber. I leave in two months." She took a breath. "I've put the shop up for sale, but if I don't get any bites, I may rent to another barber."

Lesley was deadly silent, her eyes wide and unblinking, obviously thinking, *I was so not expecting that.* Her lips compressed, and she swallowed convulsively. Because she considered herself an unlovely crier, Lesley typically went to great lengths not to weep in public. Now tears filled her eyes.

Gabby's chest clutched. *Okay. First family member I've told.... It's going well, I think.*

"I'm going to need your help, Les," she said, reaching across the table to pat her sister-in-law's wrist. "I'm going to tell the family Sunday night. I want your support. I suspect Mom's going to freak out a little."

"Your mom is going to freak out *a lot.* So's your dad.

And the girls will— Oh, Gabs. Are you sure this is the right thing to do?"

"You said I should kick my life into gear."

"I said you should have sex, not move to the Pacific Ocean." Lesley blew her nose into a paper napkin. "You won't even have a zip code."

Gabby rubbed Lesley's arm. "Not while the ship is moving. But maybe I'll have sex with some great guy who will romance me across the high seas then ask me to have his children and settle down in a house on Moon Lake. We'll host fabulous family get-togethers, and Kate and Natalie will frolic with my children along waterfront property. How's that?"

Lesley gave a watery laugh. "That's all right." She sighed, took several fortifying sips of coffee then rallied as Gabby hoped she would. "You'll need a makeover." She snuffled. "Total. You can't get on a singles' cruise with nothing but running shoes and blue jeans in your suitcase."

Gabby did have other wardrobe items, purchased the last time she'd tried to make herself over—for Dean. Then, her goal had been to liberate her "true self." This time, she was totally willing to assume someone else's true self. The self of a woman who lived life to the fullest and had never seen *Jerry Maguire* or heard Tom Cruise tell Renee Zellweger, "You complete me," which had probably depressed more singles than any other phrase in the history of spoken language.

Since Lesley's help was both required and desired for the mandated makeover, Gabby nodded agreeably. "Check."

While Lesley enumerated the myriad other activities necessary to become cruise-worthy—ballroom dance instruction, makeup lessons, bikini-ready exercise program, waxing—Gabby remembered that she used to sit in this very diner when she was a girl, imagining the day she would eat here with her husband and children, cutting hamburgers in half for small hands, intercepting straws as they jetted across the table, wiping milk shake spills…and smiling at her man, her very best friend, as they laughed together over the chaos called life and reaffirmed with their eyes alone that they were still crazy in love.

Despite what she'd said to Les about meeting someone, moving into a house nearby and having babies, Gabby knew she didn't have the heart to perpetuate that fantasy anymore. This time she wanted to reach for a brass ring she could actually close her slightly chubby fingers around.

Travel. Excitement. Dancing on the middle of the Pacific Ocean under a sky smattered with stars—that was within her grasp. And there might be a man, eventually. She no longer required a be-all and end-all romance. She would accept it if the universe brought her someone…nice. Lively and fun. And maybe it wouldn't last longer than the cruise, but, hey, compared to another twenty years loving someone who didn't love her back—

It would be plenty.

"What do you mean, you know he's back? You've been in touch with him?"

Gabby cornered her brother, Ben, in the kitchen of their parents' home as their bi-regular Sunday-night-supper-and-Crazy-Eights tournament got under way.

Thirteen months younger than Gabby, Ben was still single, lived over an hour away in Bend and played the field with a success that rivaled George Clooney's, but he usually managed to come home for Crazy Eights Sundays. And for the food.

"Don't your girlfriends feed you?" Gabby asked, tugging on his sleeve to capture his attention and save the relish tray from demolition.

Ben popped two stuffed olives in his mouth before turning to lean against the kitchen counter. Lazily crossing his ankles, he winked. "That's not why I date them, Gabrielle. Did Mom make rolls?"

"Ben." She gritted her teeth. "I'm asking you a question. Have you been in touch with Caleb Wells for a long time?"

Possessed of the trademark Coombs red hair, but in a much darker, more auburn hue, Ben was too handsome and too chill for his own good. Their parents had always said that if a major earthquake hit Oregon, Ben would find out about it two days later on the evening news. He did everything on Ben time, including answering direct questions.

"What's a long time?" he murmured now, eyeing the refrigerator as if the decision to walk over and examine its contents merited further deliberation.

"For cripe's sake." Gabby fished more olives from a jar and plunked them next to the gherkins on the neon-orange plastic tray her mother had left out for her. "Two months. Have you been in touch longer than two months?"

Ben's green eyes examined the pot lights their parents had recently installed in the kitchen ceiling. "Two months sounds about right."

"How did he find you? Facebook?"

"No, he phoned. Dylan gave him my number."

"Dylan? He's been in touch with Dylan?"

Ben shrugged. Reaching for a jar of roasted peanuts, he unscrewed the lid and shook out a handful. "He may have gotten in contact with Jeremy first. I'm not sure."

"What?" At the mention of their youngest brother,

Gabby upset an olive that rolled across the counter and onto the floor. "Why didn't anyone tell me? What about Mom and Dad? Did Cal contact them, too?"

Crunching peanuts, Ben squeezed one eye shut, peering at his sister as if viewing her under a microscope. "Have you considered tranquilizers for this condition, Gabrielle, because, you know…" He sailed his hand like an airplane a few inches above his head. "Over the top." He tossed a peanut in the air, catching it in his mouth. "What's the problem, anyway? As I recall, you didn't care one way or the other when Cal disappeared."

Lowering her eyes, Gabby grabbed a towel to mop up olive juice. "I don't like surprises, that's all."

"Hmm." The doorbell rang, and, brushing the salt off his hands, Ben headed toward the doorway. "I hope Mom and Dad do."

"What?" Gabby said, looking after her brother's retreating form, but he either didn't hear her or didn't bother to respond and continued out the door.

Gabby remained in the kitchen, finishing the relish tray and wondering what was the matter with her. Ben was right: Her reaction to Cal Wells was over the top. In all likelihood he'd had so many, er, partners since her that he barely remembered he'd once spread a Navajo blanket beneath a giant oak and had seen her, the girl he'd practically grown up with, naked in the moonlight.

Gabby ate an olive. And then a gherkin.

Cal wouldn't mention that night to anyone in her family. Would he?

Shaking her head, she dismissed her own anxieties. Because, come on, even if he did mention it, they were all adults, right?

She put three more olives in her mouth.

Please, God, I will do anything. Don't let him mention it.

She couldn't imagine having one of her brothers or—*please strike me dead first*—her parents finding out she'd begged Cal to make love to her.

Eeeeyeesh. What a sparkling romantic history—unrequited love with Dean and embarrassing teenage sex with Cal.

Her new life couldn't start soon enough.

Picking up the relish tray, she headed for the living room where her family was assembled. Her brother Dylan and his girlfriend, Julie, were the recent arrivals, which meant everyone but Jeremy, who was backpacking across Ireland with a friend from grad school, was present. For the moment, she had to push aside the problem of Caleb and concentrate on the news she had for her family.

A florist by trade, Julie was handing their mother a vase of summer blooms.

"Those are gorgeous, Julie!" Lesley called out from the floor, where she and her two daughters were playing The Bee Game. "Dylan, please marry her so we can get a family discount on lilies. I love stargazer lilies." She leaned back to see her husband, who was on the sofa, sharing a beer with his father. "You're taking notes, right?"

"Stargazer lilies." Eric nodded. "Check."

Smiling, Gabby set the relish tray on the coffee table and went to hug Dylan and the lovely woman he'd been dating for almost two years. "The flowers are glorious. And you should marry my brother. However, unlike my opportunistic sister-in-law, I would love you even if you had only yourself to offer," Gabby said as she took the flowers from her mother.

Behind her, Lesley snorted. "Suck up."

"Suck up," Lesley and Eric's four-year-old daughter, Natalie, sang. "Suck up, Aunt Gabby!"

Eric nodded to his wife. "Nicely done, honey."

The laughter helped soothe Gabby's skipping nerves. She'd agreed with Lesley that she should tell her family about her plans at the top of the evening, just dive in, since the Coombses liked to process information for a long time and sometimes quite loudly. Telling them before dinner (the alternative being to mention it as she was backing out of the driveway) would be the mature thing to do.

Dive in.

Undigested olives and the beat of her pounding heart filled her throat. "Uh, excuse me, everyone," she began. "I have some news, and I think it's best if I—"

The doorbell rang.

Thank you God, thank you, thank you.

"I'll get it," Gabby offered brightly. Pretending not to notice the face Lesley made at her, she raced for the door.

Shifting the flowers to the crook of her left arm, she opened the door with a smile that was perky as heck.

It lasted an entire four seconds.

Staring at the person on her parents' threshold, she almost dropped the vase she was holding.

Noooo. Seriously, universe?

"Don't just stand there. Let him in, Gabs." Ben's sardonic voice nudged her. And then it clicked.

"You're Ben's surprise."

Caleb, dressed in another crisp suit, this time navy blue, gave her a faintly apologetic smile. "Hello, Gabrielle."

The deep timbre of his voice sounded disturbingly intimate.

"Who is it?" her mother queried from the other side of the room.

"Ben thought my showing up might be a nice surprise

for your parents," Caleb spoke softly, for Gabby's ears alone. "If it's going to ruin your night, though, I can say hello and go. Save visiting for another time."

"Of course not," she protested automatically, feeling lower than a snake, because, yes, she would *love* for him to make her night easier by leaving.

I am a butterfly, not a caterpillar, she reminded herself. *I can handle this.*

Retrieving her smile, she stepped to the side so Cal could enter, noticing for the first time that he held a bottle of wine. Fancy stuff, not the zipped-into-Sherm's-Queen-Bee-while-the-motor-was-still-running variety. Tucked beneath his arm was a large box of truffles that probably cost as much as Gabby's sofa. In the past, Cal had made her mother small gifts—carvings out of wood and music CDs he'd burned off her brother Eric's system—saving his earned money for essentials. She may have been the same old Gabby, but he was certainly not the same Caleb.

As he entered the living room, the people inside the house fell silent. Except for Ben, who had known Caleb was coming over, and Dylan, who had already spoken to him, Gabby sensed that her family was experiencing the same shock she'd felt.

Stealing a glance at the surprise guest, Gabby saw a muscle twitch beside his left eye. A smile seemed to be fighting against his lips' desire to remain in a straight line. Cal was nervous about his reception here tonight. He had, after all, disappeared from the lives of the family that had cared for him more than his own.

Seeing him look so vulnerable, Gabby's heart squeezed uncomfortably.

Before she made a clear decision to act, she plucked the chocolate box from him and—oh, what the hell—looped her arm through his. "Look, everybody," she said, turning toward the room. "Cal's home."

Finally, exclamations—and a gasp from her mother—circled the room. There seemed to be a brief time delay and then Coombses surrounded them. Nancy began to cry, enveloping the boy she had practically raised since puberty in a mother's always-welcoming arms. Cal said hello to Eric and Lesley and the girls. Lesley made big *Did-you-know-he-was-going-to-be-here* eyes at Gabby. Dylan waited his turn to have Cal greet Julie.

The prodigal son had come home.

About to escape to the dining room to put the vase in the center of the table, Gabby looked up and caught Cal's gaze seeking hers above her family's heads. He didn't say thank you, but she understood just the same. And then he did the thing that was so rare for the Cal Wells she remembered: He smiled openly. Boyishly. A little awed.

For a moment, she saw him as the young man who'd spent a good part of his early teen years offering to do chores for her mother and defending Gabby from her brothers' roughhousing. The kid who never took the Coombses' hospitality for granted.

Surprised by a sudden rush of nostalgia or sentiment or some dang thing, Gabby swallowed against the tears that filled her throat. Never one to cry copiously, she was surprised at the waterworks that turned on with the slightest provocation lately.

When Cal turned his head to respond to something her mother asked, Gabby moved off to set the flowers in the dining room and deposit Cal's gifts in the kitchen. The problem, she realized, was that she suddenly felt a strong pull to be part of something which she would very soon be leaving behind.

Nancy's expert nose told her when dinner was ready,

and she enlisted her daughter's help in ushering everyone into the dining room. Seated around a long pine table that was at least half as wide as it was long, the Coombses commenced serving themselves with an orchestral clinking of serving spoons against bowls, and lots of chatter. Gabby had long figured out that her family would make any authority on etiquette shudder, but she loved their casual, rowdy dinners.

Gabby hoped to seat herself next to her sister-in-law, but Lesley's daughters clamored to sit on either side of her, and Eric sat next to them. Gabby moved toward Ben next, but he wanted to talk to Dylan and slipped into the seat beside him and Julie. Which, of course, left only her and Caleb standing while the others started helping themselves to the home-cooked food.

"A bit like musical chairs, isn't it?" Cal cocked a brow.

Rats. He'd noticed her avoidance maneuvers. "I'm happy to sit next to you," she lied, nodding toward the two empty seats at her father's end of the table.

"You're not happy about it at all." He laughed. "But I forgive you."

Gabby walked to the chair Cal held out. As she sank into it, he murmured, "Our reunion didn't go too well the other morning. I owe you an apology."

Surprised, she shrugged. "Forget it." *Forget everything, please. Especially the part about having sex with your favorite family's desperate daughter.*

Gabby plunked into her seat as Cal slid the chair toward the table then took his place next to her. "I'd like a moment alone, to talk," he said quietly.

Alone? "Tonight?" she squeaked.

Cal shook out his napkin, set it in his lap then turned toward her, eyes glittering with wry amusement. "Tonight would be good, yes."

Before she could respond, Ben passed her a bowl of rice pilaf, and her father boomed, "So, Caleb, what are you doing for a living?" Frank eyed the navy suit and well-groomed hands of the man who had been his hired hand on numerous occasions. "You don't look like a farmer."

Because the comment held more than a whiff of disappointment, Gabby's brothers snickered. "All right!" approved Dylan, leaning forward to peer at his brothers. "Eric, Ben, we may be off the hook. Dad can hassle Caleb now about his career."

"I don't hassle you," grumbled Frank. "You boys have fine jobs. But this farm is in your family, and someone ought to work it when I'm gone. Too many independent farmers are being run out of business these days." He did a double take into the bowl Caleb passed him and sniffed. "What is this?"

"Rice," Gabby offered.

"It's brown."

"It's good for you," Nancy scolded from the opposite end of the table, her plump arms supporting a platter of steaming corn on the cob. "Eat it." She confided to Lesley in a loud whisper, "The doctor says he needs more fiber, but he refuses to eat oat bran."

Lesley nodded back. "Fiber. Can't live with it, can't live without it." Catching Gabby's eye, she winked. "Just like men."

"Thanks, honey," Eric murmured.

Gabby smiled weakly, accepting a large, heavy ceramic bowl of homegrown string beans from Ben on her left. As she struggled to balance the dish while forking up vegetables, Caleb pulled the bowl from her hands and held it so she could serve herself more easily. "Atta girl," he commended in a whisper. "String beans are loaded with fiber."

Gabby glanced up to catch his wink, surprised by how much he was enjoying himself. His forehead was relaxed. She recalled noticing on several occasions years ago that Cal's brow was furrowed every time she saw him at school, but in her parents' home, it smoothed out. Softened. He relaxed here.

The fact that he'd lost touch with her family had surprised her years ago, and in some ways it still did.

How worried her mother had been when Cal had dropped out of sight, choosing not to return from college to share either Thanksgiving or Christmas that first year, despite the fact that he'd spent the previous five holidays with the Coombses. Eventually, her parents had accepted that he'd moved on, had wanted to build a life of his own, probably, away from the community that had given him as much pain as pleasure.

After their night together, he'd come to the house only that one miserable time; other than that, she and Cal had avoided each other like the plague the rest of the summer. Most of the time, Gabby was able to convince herself he'd walked away from that sultry July night unscathed, just a teenage boy with raging hormones and a gaffe under his belt. *Whoops, shouldn't have slept with the Coombses' virgin daughter. Mustn't let that happen again.*

No biggie.

But sometimes she wondered whether he'd felt more guilt than she credited him with, and that was when she felt the weight of their secret. He hadn't known she was a virgin, after all. Maybe he felt he'd betrayed her parents' trust and hadn't wanted to face them. Maybe he was so immensely sorry they'd…you know…that he'd run out of town. *Ugh.*

The first few years after he'd left, she'd actually worried about him, despite trying not to think about him at all. Cal had always held himself apart from other people, especially at school, where he had been the quintessential tough-kid loner. Had he found people to belong to after he left for college? And, if not, was she the reason he had denied himself the comfort of a family to come home to?

Not a pretty thought.

She sneaked a peek at him. Strong jaw locked into position, he watched her family closely. Gabby remembered that about him now, how observant he had been, often studying his surroundings as if life were a documentary. What, she wondered now, had he been looking for?

"So what is it you do, Caleb?" Frank tried again, reaching for the bowl of string beans and heaping them onto his plate next to a tiny serving of brown rice.

"I'm a civil engineer," Cal answered, turning his full attention to her father. "I attended graduate school in Illinois, interned with a company in Chicago then stayed on."

"Chicago." Ben was mightily impressed. "I've heard it's a great city. Hot women." He waggled his brows at his mother, who pestered him constantly to mend his playboy ways and bring home "a nice girl, not someone in a skirt cut up to her yoo-hoo."

Frank was less impressed than his son with Caleb's choice of venues. "Chicago? What do they grow there?"

"Ideas, sir. I spent a lot of time on the thirtieth floor, thinking."

"Huh. We can use more engineers right here in Oregon, *doing* something to increase crop production for the small farmer while politicians sit on their keisters in Washington, D.C., *thinking* up new ways to plow us under—"

"Dad…."

"Frank."

"It isn't Cal's fault, after all."

"Actually, Mr. Coombs, I hope to accomplish exactly what you're talking about in my new job. I'm looking forward to trading in suits for jeans and work boots."

Frank's bushy brows rose in happy surprise. "Is that so? You'll be working in farming?"

"And other land-use issues, yes."

"Based out of where?"

"I may have to drive a few miles for my fieldwork, but my home base will be right here in Honeyford. I found a rental with a six-month lease. I went downtown to sign the agreement this morning, as a matter of fact. After that, if everything works out, I hope to buy."

About to spoon glazed carrots onto her plate, Gabby whipped around to look at Caleb, spilling carrots onto her mother's—thankfully, vinyl—tablecloth in the process. Cal was moving back to Honeyford? As in…permanently?

A surge of adrenaline made her dizzy. What if Cal got chummy with her brothers again, hung out at the farm with her parents? Granted, reality TV provided bigger scandals than sex between two kids who had grown up together, but if the story unraveled into thread after thread of humiliating detail then the middle of the ocean would not be far enough away for her to hide. Her mother liked to pretend that Ben was still just a virgin who liked to flirt. Nancy would not deal well with the news that her daughter had flung herself at the boy she and Frank considered their surrogate son.

And then it occurred to her there might be one thing more embarrassing than her parents' finding out she'd once had sex with Cal Wells: Cal finding out she hadn't been with anyone else since.

Chapter Four

"How did Main Street strike you after living in Chicago, Cal? I don't think there have been too many changes in twenty years," Lesley asked, too busy convincing her younger daughter to take the olives off her fingers to realize that her best friend was drowning in flop sweat on the other side of the dining room table. "Are most of the businesses the same ones you remember?"

"I think they are," Cal acknowledged. "I was hoping there wouldn't be many changes. Though I guess eventually I'll have to get used to the fact that nothing stays exactly the same."

Oh, crud. Her eyes flew to his. *I haven't told them yet,* she tried to communicate. *Say nothing!*

"Did you use Honeytown Realty?" Frank asked. "John Delmus owns it. He and I have played a hole or two of golf in our day."

"Yes, I did, and John was great." Splitting his Parker House roll, Cal idly buttered the halves. "He mentioned he expected a few changes to the downtown area soon. Still, I have to admit I was surprised when I realized Gab—*baah!*"

Gabby couldn't help it; she kicked him under the table. Maybe a little too hard.

As Cal's muscles reflexively contracted, he squeezed the soft roll in his hand into a lumpy dough ball.

Frank raised a gray brow. "What's wrong?"

Setting the bread aside, Cal reached for his water. "Injured ankle." His eyes cut Gabby's way.

As the talk around the table resumed, thankfully focusing on other topics, Cal leaned toward her. "Was that necessary?"

"Yes, it was." Stretching her lips into a reasonable facsimile of a smile, she spoke under her breath. "I haven't told them yet."

His brows rose. Beneath his breath, he uttered an unwholesome word. "When are you planning to?"

"When the time is right."

"That's playing with fire."

He sounded like Lesley, who earlier had reminded Gabby that in small towns, secrets tended to spread like head lice—very quickly and exactly where you didn't want them to go. Feeling the pressure, she admitted, "I'm thinking about telling them during dessert tonight." Her stomach clenched. An ulcer could not be far off.

Cal nodded. "I suppose there's a poetic sense in breaking the news over Snickerdoodles. Make the moment bittersweet."

Gabby felt herself blanch, and Cal grimaced. "Sorry. Again. I didn't intend that the way it sounded." His mouth quirked regretfully. "Regardless of when you tell them, it'll be tough to hear. You're their linchpin, Gabby. That's all I mean. But no one can fault you for following your heart. I was wrong earlier, in the barbershop."

His voice settled over the moment like a blanket, warm and comforting, and for just an instant his gaze seemed to reach right inside her. As a teenager, Cal had been sparing with small talk, but quick to defend the people he cared about. Gabby stared at him, at a loss for a response, until Dylan tapped his water glass with a butter knife.

"Ding ding ding. It's the bonus round," he announced.

"Round what? What's he talking about?" Frank asked, poking his fork suspiciously into the salmon Nancy served as a main course. "Why are we eating fish? And this *brown* stuff." He scooted a few grains of rice around on his plate and pouted down the table at his wife. "It's Sunday. My mouth's been watering for pot roast."

"Your arteries are crying for fish," Nancy said, adding sternly, "Doctor's orders, Frank," when her husband of thirty-eight years appeared ready to protest.

Heads rose around the table. "What's wrong with your arteries, Dad?" Dylan asked, setting aside his own announcement for the time being.

Frank and Nancy traded looks. Nancy raised the eyebrows she'd penciled in earlier in the day. Frank shrugged.

A fission of foreboding zigzagged up Gabby's spine. "Mom? Dad? What's up?"

Setting her utensils gently on her plate, Nancy Coombs looked fondly around the table. "Children," she said, including everyone, "just like cars, people need maintenance, and it's time for your father to have a tune-up."

"My sixty-three-thousand-mile check." He winked. "Nothing to worry about."

Gabby couldn't help it; her heart began to pound anxiously. Poppy had suffered from high cholesterol, high blood pressure, high sugar—you name it, it was high.

He'd had his first stroke when he wasn't too much older than her father. "What does that mean exactly?"

"It means your father is having heart surgery," Nancy answered, smiling gamely at her family, but her mouth trembled. "One or two little arteries. Not the important ones."

"Not the important ones!" Gabby's exclamation was not the only one that rose in the dining room, but it was the loudest. Cal reached over and squeezed her hand. His warm touch was firm and bracing, but it failed to arrest the adrenaline that pumped through her veins.

Frank waved one of the calloused farmer's hands that had been so capable through the years. "Calm down, calm down, everybody. These days bypasses are as common as…" he waved his fork "…vasectomies."

"Awesome analogy, Dad," Ben commended.

"What's a vasss-enemy?" Kate asked Lesley as her grandmother glowered down the table and scolded, "Mixed company, Frank!"

"Now'd be a fine time to crack open that wine," Frank growled to Cal out the corner of his mouth. He smiled at his wife. "Wine's good for the heart. Right, Sweetpea?"

"Red wine," Nancy confirmed.

"Did you bring red wine, son?" Frank asked Cal.

"I brought a Syrah rose, sir."

Frank, a brewskie man, who, Gabby was certain, did not know a Syrah from a Chablis, said, "Red enough. Go get it."

Cal smiled, pushing back his chair. Rather than removing his hand from Gabby's and rising on his own, however, he closed his fingers more firmly around her, drawing her up with him. "Gabby can show me where the corkscrew and glasses are."

She wanted to refuse, but had no idea how. Besides, she had just realized that tears burned her eyes.

As they walked to the kitchen, Gabby avoided Lesley's gaze and tried unsuccessfully to slip her hand free of Cal's. Tightening his hold, he pulled her along, unerringly remembering the way to the old farmhouse-style kitchen. The big, square room hadn't changed much, and, once inside, he released her without a word. A Lucite napkin holder sat on the counter, in exactly the same spot it had occupied for as long as Gabby could remember. Cal went to it now, withdrawing a white square and passing it to her.

"It *is* a fairly common procedure these days," he said kindly.

She wiped her eyes and nose, which—*lovely*—had also started to run. "I know. It's just..."

"You're on the brink of change, but you'd rather not have too much change all at once."

Her gaze snapped to his face. "Right," she whispered.

He nodded. "I've been there. If nothing ever changed, there'd be no butterflies. Your grandfather told me that one."

She lingered on his words—one of her grandfather's favorite quotes—and on the compassion in Cal's expression. In the barbershop, it had seemed he still possessed only a narrow repertoire of expressions, but this evening...

Struggling to reconcile the boy-Cal and the man—amidst all the other things she was struggling with tonight—Gabby balled up the napkin and walked it to the garbage pail beneath the sink. Moving to her mother's utensils drawer, she rummaged through it for the corkscrew.

"Here," she said, locating the instrument and passing it to him. "It's ancient. It was a wedding present. I don't think they've used it since Eric and Lesley announced their engagement, and they opened a bottle of Purple Moon."

The hazel eyes danced as he took the corkscrew. "I like that about your parents. No pretension."

"True."

From the counter, Cal plucked the bottle of wine he'd brought and began to open it. "Imagine keeping a small wedding present like this for...what? Over thirty years?"

"Thirty-eight."

He shook his head. "I don't think I have any of my wedding presents. Maybe the toaster."

On her way to the pantry to retrieve her mother's folding stepladder, Gabby skidded to a stop and turned around. "You're married? You—you had a wedding?"

Probably there was a way to sound more ridiculous, but for now, stuttering because Cal Wells had gotten married would have to suffice.

All her life, Gabby had loved weddings, and Honeyford had been rich with them over the past several months. As glad as she was each time a man and woman found each other and pledged forever (she *was* glad for them—Girl Scout's honor), it had to be confessed that each new Honeyford nuptial pricked a tiny hole in her heart.

After Dean got married, Gabby canceled her subscription to *Modern Bride* and refused to even glance at the *Martha Stewart Living* weddings issue. (Well, perhaps she'd *peeked.* Cupcake wedding cakes—so cute!)

The thing was, Gabby had had her own wedding planned for years. She'd planned for the affair to be an homage to marriage itself. Honeyford nuptials tended to be simple, cozy affairs, usually at Honeyford Pres, or festooned with balloons at the community center, or held outdoors. Dan and Elliana Boardman had trimmed the gazebo in Doc Kingsley Memorial Park with white rose-buds and twinkle lights.

Full disclosure? Gabby had bought herself a wedding planner for her twenty-third birthday. Went all the way to a chain bookstore in Bend to get it. It was pink, covered in plush faux fur, as soft and cushiony as new love itself.

It was the one thing she hadn't been able to part with when she'd signed on for the cruise ship job and decided that a life of adventure would be far healthier than a life-time filled with nothing more than longing. So when the magazines hit the bottom of the recycle bin, the wedding planner went back into her dresser drawer, where it occasionally sent up distress signals: *I'm still here...don't for-get me....* Fortunately, the signals were growing fainter all the time.

But hearing that Cal Wells had gotten married? That stung. He'd been a classic loner in high school. He hadn't pursued girls, yet had been treated to overt flirtation from the ones who had clearly wanted to date the "bad boy." He hadn't made an effort at all as far as Gabby could see. And yet he'd found someone he loved who loved him back.

This was why she had to let go of the idea of "true love" and get on with her life. She cut men's hair day in and day out, yet with all those males in her orbit, mutual passion had never walked in and taken a seat.

Another white napkin appeared beneath her nose. "You want to talk about it?"

Dang! Her eyes were wet again. She sniffed hard.

"Nothing to talk about. One of those days."

"Mm." He stared at her, the shining eyes sober as a judge now. "Okay."

Gabby wadded her second napkin. What had she been about to do...? Oh, yeah. Retrieving her mother's folding stepladder from the pantry, she set it beneath the cabinet where the wine goblets lined up along the top shelf like debutantes awaiting their turns to dance.

"So," she said with a big, happy-for-you smile, "you're married! And moving back to Honeyford! Why? I mean, I didn't think you liked it here that much. Are you and your wife considering this a permanent move?"

Reapplying himself to the wine bottle, Cal arched a wry brow. "I've given up predicting the future. *I'm* moving back indefinitely, yes. With my daughter. My *ex*-wife has other plans."

Facts ricocheted around Gabby's head like a pinball.

He was divorced, but… "You have a daughter."

Chalk up another smile in his repertoire of expressions. This one was as clean and simple as rain in spring.

"Her name is Minna, which she sometimes loves and sometimes hates. She's ten. Bright. Kind. Smart mouth." The right side of his mouth hiked so high it almost ran into his laugh lines. "I hope you'll meet her."

"I hope so, too," Gabby murmured automatically, distracted by her own surprise. Cal had been a father for *ten years*—since he was twenty-three. "I'm sorry about you and…Minna's mother?"

"Minna's mother," he confirmed as the cork slipped sweetly from the bottle. "We were married a year before she came along, stayed married six years after then separated. The split became official two years ago."

It was more information than she'd have dared ask for and led to still more questions. In lieu of asking them, she simply repeated, "I'm sorry." Climbing the stepladder, she began removing wine glasses. "It must be so hard for all of you. And now you'll be living apart."

Cal set the wine on the counter. "We're used to it. Victoria traveled frequently for work. She accepted a position in France before the divorce was finalized."

France. So far away from Cal and their daughter. Gabby had always lived near family, had never imagined *not* living near family…until now.

Moving to her side, Cal reached for the goblets she pulled off the top shelf.

"I can do it," she protested. He was too close for comfort, his shoulder barely a couple of inches from her left breast.

"Just hand me the glasses, Gabby. It'll be safer than you trying to keep your balance when you put them on the sink. It looks like they could use a rinse, too."

For a few moments they transferred the wine goblets that rarely departed from their perch.

"So, really, why Honeyford?" she asked, genuinely curious. "I wasn't aware you had ties here anymore." That sounded a bit harsh, since the Coombses could be considered a link to his past. "I mean, your mother and aunt moved away years ago, didn't they?"

Accepting another pair of gold-rimmed goblets, Cal replied in an even voice, "They did. Family is the reason I came back, though. Your folks and Max taught me all I know about parenting."

Well. That was sweet.

"The truth is I haven't been as successful as I'd like to be at creating a family for Minna. My in-laws are good people, but…"

"What?"

"'Cuddly' is not the first word that pops to mind when you think of them."

"Ah." Did it pop to mind when he thought of the ex-wife? And if not, why'd he marry her?

Not that everyone desired a cuddly mate, she supposed, but Gabby certainly would have wanted one. It would have been a requirement: Do you promise to love, honor and cuddle so long as you both shall live?

Would there be cuddles, she wondered, with meaningless cruise sex? Would she even want cuddles in that situation?

Her mood growing vaguely duller, Gabby climbed off the stool and indicated that Cal should scoot over so she could start rinsing glasses. Instead of letting her do the job alone, he grabbed the dishtowel her mother had looped through a drawer pull.

"I'll dry."

"Thanks." She had to smile. Helpful. Her brothers—at least the bachelor bros—had an aversion to anything that smacked of housework. As they got busy, Gabby found the temerity to say, "You certainly married young. Were you very much in love?"

Together they washed and dried a goblet before he responded. "I tried my best to make it work. Maybe it's more accurate to say I was looking for love."

She didn't have the nerve to ask whether his wife had loved him. Instead, she asked, "Where is your daughter now?"

"Still with her grandparents. She's finishing up fourth grade, complaining about the private school I'm selling my blood to send her to, can't wait for summer and is actually happy we're moving."

He sounded like a dad, affection shining through the everyday complaints. "I bet she'll miss her friends, though," Gabby said.

There was another pause as Cal concentrated more than necessary on preventing water spots. Gabby wondered at his silence; to her, the comment was pretty straightforward. By ten, most girls were clinging to their BFFs.

Finally he looked up, his eyes unreadable, green glass

again instead of a hazel lake. "Minna struggles socially. She has cerebral palsy. Not the most serious form, but enough to make her feel different from her peers." His tone hardened. "It takes the hide of a rhinoceros to get through school without caring that you're different."

The hide of a rhinoceros—or a lot of love. "Do the other kids care so much?" Gabby asked.

"There are girls who have made overtures. Min seemed to be doing all right, but after her mother left..." He set one dry wineglass aside. She handed him a wet one. "She's becoming too much like me. I'd like to nip that in the bud."

"Too much like you in what way?"

"She's closing off. Afraid to talk about feelings. All the usual challenges of pre-adolescence magnified." Cal took a deep breath. "I'm hoping your family will help me, Gabby. The Coombses know more about love and making someone feel accepted than I've ever learned. Assuming they're willing to get involved, I'd love for them to be in Minna's life."

"Willing?" She laughed. "My parents will think it's Christmas every day with another kid to spoil," she told him. "They'll love it. You have nothing to worry about."

"How about where you're concerned?" His hands stilled, and he faced her head-on, his gaze probing. "Will it make you uncomfortable if you find us hanging around the farm a lot?"

Ah, the crux of the matter. "Is this what you wanted to talk to me about?"

"Partly." He set the glass aside. "But that's not all. There's another conversation that's about fifteen years overdue."

Wiping his hands, he reached for her upper arm, fingers closing around her bare skin. It was the first time he'd made contact above her wrist since that night. Gabby almost dropped the glass she was holding.

"I owe you an apology," he said. "We never talked about what happened between us. I should have made a better effort to check on you after we—"

Don't say it. Gabby felt herself grow stiff as a statue even as heat flooded every cell in her body.

The more they talked about what had happened between them, the closer he could come to uncovering the truth about what *hadn't* happened since—namely, another sexual encounter for her.

Her condition—impending rigor mortis—must have communicated itself to him, because he resorted to a euphemism. "After our encounter."

Gabby's gaze traveled to the scratches in the porcelain sink…to the frayed edge of her mother's café curtains…to the goblet dripping in her hands…anywhere to avoid looking at Cal. "Don't be silly," she murmured, "I was perfectly fine."

"I know you were fine physically." His voice turned impossibly soft and considerate. "It was your first time. I should have made sure you were okay emotionally, too."

The glass she held under the running faucet started to slip into the white porcelain sink as her fingers fumbled. Cal lunged forward to help her make the save. His fingers were flames of fire as they closed around hers.

For fifteen years she'd buried the details of that night, the way he had touched her (hungrily)…the fact that he'd seemed to know what he was doing…and her body's initial response—a dam ready to burst, with an ocean of frustrated emotion surging inside her and desire for Cal that stunned her.

Marshaling all her inner resources, she pulled the goblet from his grasp without breaking it—proving she wasn't panicked—and turned off the water. A teetotaler all her life, she eyed the open bottle of wine and imagined herself drinking half of it.

"Cal," she said, "you know, that was so long ago. It's not, um, you know...I don't think it's necessary to—"

"I have a daughter, Gabby. I'm going to expect the boy who takes her virginity to treat her afterward with the respect she deserves. I owed you that much. Not to bury my head in the sand and pretend nothing ever happened between us."

"Oh, gosh, no, that's okay." *Please. Take the ostrich approach. I love ostriches.*

They both knew he'd tried to see her the day after the event. He'd stood outside her bedroom door, whispering, his voice carrying clearly past the wood panel while she'd stood on the other side, pretending to have caught the mother of all summer colds. She could still picture the scene: His whispered urgings to open the door, her fake coughs.

She was going to hurl the olives she'd eaten earlier, no question. Suffice to say, Cal had seen her downtown later that day, and the result was that he had not tried to talk to her alone again. She'd never been certain whether it was because of what he had seen or because he'd simply moved on and couldn't be bothered to try again. Either way....

"You weren't responsible for my feelings," she told him now, determined to end this part of the conversation. "What we did wasn't really about feelings, anyway, was it?" She laughed, sounding nervous, giddy, slightly crazy to her own ears. "So you weren't responsible for mine."

She felt his stare linger a long while before he responded. "Right." From her peripheral vision, she saw him nod slowly. "Fair enough." Turning, he resumed his task with the glasses. "I suppose when you become a father to a daughter, you can't help but review how you treat women yourself. How you want your daughter to be treated. Back to topic number one then— Will you be uncomfortable if Minna and I spend time at the farm?"

Did he really think she would deny him the opportunity given what he'd told her about his daughter? "Cal, I would never get in the way of your reconnecting with my parents."

"That doesn't answer my question."

He wanted a serious answer to a serious question. She sighed. "My family has no idea what happened between us."

"I gathered."

"I don't know about you, but I'd like to keep it that way."

"That's your primary concern?"

"I think so."

"All right." He nodded. "I'm not a big fan of secrets. They're like cheese—the longer you keep them, the moldier they get. But I'll honor your request."

She smiled. He sounded like Poppy.

"I have a request of my own," he added.

"What is it?"

"I'd like it if you could stop looking guilty and nervous when I'm around. We managed to coexist pretty peacefully a long time ago. Think we could do it again?"

His expression was so earnest, so devoid of any mocking or wryness despite the still-watchful intensity of his eyes, that she nodded.

"I'm not going to be around much longer, anyway," she reminded him and herself.

"So you are planning to leave town after you sell Honey

Comb's?" He swept the towel off his shoulder and resumed drying the last of the wine goblets.

"I'm leaving town even if the shop doesn't sell right away. I already have a position with a cruise line," she said, pleased to be able to report that her life had jumped tracks. "I leave in September."

The subtle rise of his brows was the only indication that she'd caught him off guard. "Good for you," he murmured.

He accepted the last of the wine goblets, swirled the dish towel around it and set it aside. "Looks like we're ready to take these into the dining room." He handed her the towel so she could dry her hands.

"Thanks."

Picking up the wine bottle and several of the glasses by their stems, he started toward the doorway.

"Uh, Cal?" she said. "Remember, my parents don't know yet about Honey Comb's or that I'm planning to leave. Under the circumstances—my dad needing surgery—I may break it to them more slowly than I'd planned. Tell them about the shop first."

Pausing, he looked back to study her carefully. "I hope you won't let anything get in the way of your dream."

"I won't."

He gazed at her a moment longer, then headed for the doorway, hesitating one last time. "By the way, Gabrielle, for the record—*I'm* not embarrassed that we had sex. Not a bit." There went the right side of his mouth again, curling slowly. "I'm only sorry I didn't know as much about making love then as I do now. Our relationship that summer might have lasted longer than a single night."

Chapter Five

"Nice neighbors, huh, Min?" Cal watched his ten-year-old daughter dissect a chunk of beef with her fork, examining it as if she were a CSI on a hot case. "Mrs. Gould brought us enough dinner to feed an army."

"Good idea, Dad. The army can have my share." Looking relieved, Minna let her fork clatter to her plate and sat back, her dark brows drawing together—preteen storm clouds heralding another angry evening. "Who eats beef stew in the summer, anyway?"

"People who are grateful for a good meal." Cal issued the reprimand even though he knew it would elicit eye rolling or the erection of some other wall between him and the young woman who used to grin or giggle at practically every pearl that fell from his mouth. The good old days.

"Min," he tried again, "what's up? We've been here a week, and you get angrier every day. Talk to me, butter-fly." He called her by the nickname he'd used since she was four years old and decided she *was* a butterfly. Unable to walk without help due to the cerebral palsy that had been diagnosed when she was a toddler, his gorgeous smiling girl had asked him over and over to pick her up and "fly me around, Dada!" While Cal had lifted her as high as he could, she had fluttered her arms. Each time they played the game, they were able to forget for a short while that Minna had never run across a playground or spontaneously raced to her daddy's open arms. Cal had loved giving her the freedom of movement her physical challenges didn't allow.

He ached to give her the freedom now to talk about what was bugging her, but this parenting moment felt like scaling an active volcano compared to playing butterfly.

"Lay it on me," he tried, anyway. "What's not working for you here?"

With her large hazel eyes and long black hair tied off her fair face, Minna resembled an American Girl doll. She had her mother's cosmetically perfect nose and full lips, but the resemblance ended with the physical. Victoria's chilly personality seemed to be the result of a long-ago decision not to feel anything too deeply. Minna, on the other hand, was a cauldron of preteen need and confusion. Cal comforted himself that as long as they talked about things, they'd be okay.

Minna looked at him as if the answer to his question were as obvious as one plus one equals two. "What *is* working for me here?" she complained vociferously. "This place is like some weird salute to the golden age of television. It's like the longest *Leave It To Beaver* episode in history."

"Hey, you love the golden age of television," he couldn't resist pointing out. He and Minna had a library of classic TV.

"I like Lucille Ball, Dad. She was inventive. This place is totally white bread."

He couldn't argue there. "Look, Min, comparing Honeyford to Chicago is like weighing a marshmallow against the world's greatest chocolate. But marshmallows have their own charm, right?" When his daughter merely stared, Cal closed his eyes. He was sucking at the wise father role.

"The things people like to do around here are boring and stupid," she complained.

Cal stared at the little girl who had previously been devoid of a single judgmental bone in her body, except when she judged herself. Had he truly made a mistake moving them here? Or were they simply in the awkward adjustment phase? More to the point, was parenting honestly a job at which a mere mortal could excel?

"Babe," he said, remembering parenting rule number one: Keep your voice calm. "Give me something concrete to work with. You've been here a week. What *exactly* do you hate?" He nodded to her untouched plate. "Besides the stew. Tell me every rotten thing about this place."

Minna's gaze slid away from his. Stiffening her arms against the table, she pushed herself back in the dining room chair until it tilted, a dangerous maneuver, but Caleb bit his tongue and waited for her to speak.

"Why do I have to sleep downstairs? The bedrooms are upstairs."

Because that had nothing to do with the town as far as Caleb could see, it took him a moment to shift gears. "We talked about this. I wouldn't have chosen a two-story house, but it was the only one for rent that was walking distance to downtown. I figured you'd like that. When we're ready to buy, we'll look for a single level. And as soon as we get a lift installed on the staircase—"

"I am not using a lift! And if you put one in this house, I'm leaving. I mean it."

"Min—"

"I hate this house already. It's so…yellow. If you put a gimpmobile on the staircase, I'm out of here. I can get up the stupid stairs on my own! Not without looking like a total freakazoid, but I can do it, and I don't want to sleep in the living room!"

Cal could see that with everything in her, Minna wanted to jump from the table and run off to feel whatever she was feeling in private. The best she could do, however, was to get herself onto her feet on the second try, then grab her crutches and exit the room as quickly as she was able in her distinctive bobbing toe walk.

Sighing, he set his fork on the plate. The stew was great, the thought behind it touching, but he, too, had lost his appetite. Picking up his plate, he rose to clear the table, but abandoned the task when the doorbell rang.

Please be Barry Sears, he thought, recalling all the how-to-raise-your-kid books by that author and others that had decorated his nightstand during the early years, especially once he'd realized he was going to be traveling the parenting road largely on his own.

On the way to the door, Cal glanced at the boxes stacked against the living room wall and made a solemn promise to eradicate half of them this weekend. The day after having dinner at the Coombses' home, he had flown to Chicago, picked up his daughter, made arrangements to have their belongings transported to Oregon, and got Minna settled at a day camp for the summer. He'd felt as if he was pretty much on top of things. The camp was for "normies"—Minna's word, not his—and she had seemed excited about the opportunity to ride horses and swim in a lake. What had happened to sour her first week there?

Cal answered the bell so deep in thought about Minna, he didn't even wonder who had come to call. Surprise filled him after he opened the door. "Gabby!"

"Hi. Sorry to bother you during the dinner hour. My mother's afraid you might not know how to cook, so she sent a roasted chicken, a pan of lasagna and probably fifteen side dishes. One for each year you've been gone."

A chuckle rose from Cal's gut, and, damn, it felt good given the rest of his week. He hadn't seen Gabby since the night at her parents' house and would never have expected her to show up on his doorstep.

"So you're only the messenger?" he asked, reaching out to relieve her of the bag she held up as if it were show-and-tell.

"Mom plays Bunko tonight. Eric is with his family. Ben, being God's gift to women, cannot be bothered on Fridays, and Dylan and Julie are currently useless to anyone but each other."

"In other words, maternal coercion brought you to my door."

"Pretty much."

"Come in."

Gabby held up a hand. "No can do. First rule of good delivery service—Never cross the recipient's threshold."

Relieved of the grocery bag, Gabby had put her hands in the back pockets of her jeans. She wore a sleeveless ivory T-shirt with a candy-striped barber pole and the words "Honey Comb's Barbershop, Old-Fashioned and Proud of It." Her casual stance made the T-shirt stretch across her bosom, which made Cal remember that she had the kind of curves a man could take his time tracing.

Saying "thanks" and "so long" on the threshold was the wise thing to do, but he ignored wisdom.

"First rule of good friendship," he replied, "come meet my daughter."

"Are we going to be friends?"

The thick red curls that had always mesmerized him were loosely bound in a knot at the back of her head. Soft flyaway coils made her look, adorably, as if she'd been working hard, rushing all day. He wanted to offer her a drink. And a neck massage.

"Yeah, friends. That's what we were before. Right?"

Stepping back, he waited for her to make her decision. If she came in, he would offer the drink, not the neck massage.

"Sure," she agreed after a moment, head bobbing as if she wasn't sure at all. "I'll come in, but just for a minute. I'd like to meet your daughter."

"Great. I think she's in the kitchen."

Gabby crossed the threshold, and they hovered awkwardly inside the doorway until Cal remembered it was his house and, therefore, his first move. "Good news about Dylan and Julie, hmm?" he said, heading toward the kitchen. The night they had all gathered at her parents' house, her brother Dylan and his girlfriend had announced their engagement and that—surprise!—they were having a baby, too. "Once they got past the shock, your mother and father seemed excited."

"Beyond. My mother is tracing our family tree online so she can phone more people."

"It deflected a bit from your news, didn't it?"

"An added bonus. She and my father are working so hard to make sure this wedding happens before the baby happens that they haven't had a lot of time to worry about me. My dad came to the shop for 'trims' twice this week—which is more than I've seen him in the past four months—and did a lot of heavy sighing while he was there. Mom averages five quick phone calls a day to ask if I'm serious about leaving and to remind me that the Coombses have a history of seasickness. I'd say I'm getting off pretty easily."

A wry smile tickled Gabby's lips and pulled on Cal's heart.

If asked last week, he would have bet Gabby was going to postpone giving her family the news that she was leaving. Faced with the announcement of her father's impending surgery and her brother's impending marriage, she'd have been well within her rights to save her news for another time.

But she'd manned up. Or womaned up. Clinking a dessert spoon against her wineglass, she'd told them Honey Comb's was for sale. Sweat had popped in tiny, heart-wrenching beads along her forehead, and Cal had almost reached up to squeeze her hand. But it was her life, not his. She was moving on. Alone.

And that put a period on any sentence in his head that might have begun, "Gabby and Caleb…." Not that he'd returned to Honeyford believing that Gabby was going to be part of his future. Nope. But sometimes it was better not only to shut a door, but to drywall over the damn thing, too.

"Sorry about the boxes," he told her as she followed him through the living and dining rooms.

"Not a problem. Wow, it smells good in here." In the determinedly cheerful yellow dining room, she stopped walking and looked at the table, set with the dishes of stew they'd hardly touched. "Do you cook?"

"I've learned how to do a few things out of necessity over the years—breakfast for dinner, a jar of spaghetti sauce over chicken." He nodded to the table. "Nothing like that, though. My neighbor Irene Gould took pity on us."

"Ah, Irene." Gabby nodded fondly. "When Claire lived here, she would bake, and Irene would cook. It was a dangerous place to hang out."

"You know Claire Kingsley, the owner here?"

"We're good friends." Gabby's long fingers trailed over the back of one of the modern chairs Cal had shipped from his condo. He knew his furniture was stylistically out of place in this house, but the glass-topped dining table seemed particularly mismatched to the flowered wallpaper and gold light fixture in this room.

He tightened his hold on the handled shopping bag. Maybe his furniture was simply a barometer. Maybe he and Minna didn't belong here any more than they had in Chicago, and this move would play out as a dumb-ass, single dad's last-ditch effort to give his kid a feeling of family.

"You're in the middle of dinner," Gabby said. "I can meet Minna another—"

"No!" Hearing his own anxiety, Cal rubbed a hand over his head. He'd nearly made her jump, but the thought of being alone again with his concerns held all the appeal of an evening dodging bullets. "You're not interrupting anything," he told Gabby. "We weren't as hungry as we thought, so…" He shrugged then asked, "Are you hungry?"

"Me?" She shook her head. "I just got off work, and I usually…go for a run before dinner. Thanks, anyway."

"A run." He nodded, smiling. "That sounds good. I

haven't had time lately. Well…" He gestured toward the closed kitchen door. "Let's see what Min is up to."

I usually go for a run before dinner.

What a lie! Gabby cringed as she followed Cal through the swinging door and into the kitchen. What she "usually" did before dinner was have a little snack. However, in an effort not to be *her* anymore, she had embarked on her head-to-toe makeover by going for *a* run—just one— after work on Monday, four days ago. She was still recovering.

She'd pounded down Old Highway 138 until sweat had spurt from every pore, her stomach had cramped and every joint below her waist had threatened to go on strike. That was after half a mile. After pushing herself a half mile more, she'd turned around and, praying no one she knew would drive by, jog-limped the mile back to town, bought a smoothie at the general store and collapsed on the couch as soon as she got home.

Lesley had typed up an agenda for Gabby's makeover, so she'd chosen less…violent options for the rest of the week. Tonight, her task was to post her profile on an on-line dating site in an effort to secure a dance partner/ potential date—strictly, Lesley assured her, for practice.

Makeovers were exhausting.

Stepping inside the sunny-yellow kitchen, Gabby remembered the simpler days when she'd hung out here, taste-testing Claire's killer pastries, moaning about her weight and plotting ways to make Dean notice her. Good times.

She'd also raced around the kitchen table, playing "stampeding herd of buffaloes" with Claire's sons and bouncing baby Rosalind on her knee while talking in a squeaky voice. There had been an empty space in her heart that awaited a man and child to fill it, and with every drooly giggle Claire's adorable daughter had offered, Gabby had felt the empty space grow bigger, roomier, more ready.

After a while, though, as she watched other singles become couples and then families, Gabby had begun to picture herself as a lone bird, feathering a nest that remained perennially empty. That image was too pathetic, which was why she'd decided to fill the empty space in her heart with other things—work, friends, adventure and someday a romance or two. She'd be like Kate Winslet's character in *Titanic*—independent, trailblazing, true to herself… minus the sea tragedy, lost lover and stolen gem issues.

She was going to attack that dating website the moment she got home.

"Minna, I have someone I'd like you to meet. This is Gabrielle Coombs. We grew up together here in Honeyford."

Cal's calm voice brought her back to the present, directing her attention to the sad-looking girl who sat at the kitchen table, using a spoon to scoop the white filling from a Suzy Q.

"Hi," Gabby said, captured immediately by how alone the girl looked. "Really glad to meet you, Minna."

Hearing that Cal had a daughter was one thing. Seeing the proof was something else again. The young girl didn't really look like Cal, save for watchful hazel eyes that did bear a striking resemblance to his. If Minna resembled her mother, then Caleb Wells had obviously fallen for a beauty. Unfortunately, good looks were apparently not aiding Minna's transition from Chicago to Honeyford. Not yet, anyway. She looked miserable.

Beside her, Gabby felt Cal's tension climb as he watched his daughter eat mystery filling from a packaged cupcake when a perfectly good dinner sat virtually untouched on their dining room table.

"Min," he prompted when his daughter continued to stare at Gabby without speaking.

"Oh, right. Sorry," she mumbled, more caught off guard than certifiably rude. "I didn't know my dad still had friends here. I mean, I thought they all moved or died or something. Hi."

On the verge of the best laugh she'd had in days, Gabby peeked at Cal. He seemed flummoxed.

"I take it you haven't met too many adults since you've been here," Gabby guessed.

"Just the woman who brought stew. Mostly I've met kids at stupid summer camp." Minna shot a hasty glance at her father. "Sorry."

Cal frowned. "What's wrong with the camp, Min?" His tone was genuinely concerned and also bore more than a hint of parental frustration. "You've been dying to ride horses and swim. I thought you'd love it there."

All her life, it seemed, Gabby had felt like the girl who didn't possess half the life skills other people did, socially speaking. But clearly she knew more than Cal when it came to girls and camp. If Minna felt she didn't fit in, then all the horses and lake swimming in the world wouldn't turn camp into the summer paradise parents liked to picture. Spying the single crutch that leaned against the table, Gabby wondered if Minna's disability was the problem.

"Are you going to Camp Buford?" Gabby guessed.

"Yeah." That *yeah* conveyed more meaning than several sentences would have.

"Mmm," Gabby murmured, her tone noncommittal. "I went there. Four summers in a row. Do you know that it's named after a real person? Olive Ann Buford." She stepped forward, reached for a Suzy Q from the open box on the table and removed the wrapper. "Buford donated the land. She used to visit the camp for an overnight each summer well into her eighties. She wore her old camp uniform and ate these giant dill pickles. We called it Camp Burpford for obvious reasons."

Minna started to smile, a tiny hitch that only touched one side of her lips. She really was like Cal.

A strangely satisfying sense of victory made Gabby's veins buzz. Raising the white-filled chocolate cupcake to her mouth, she held off at the last minute. "You know what? I'm hungrier than I thought. Maybe I'll save this for later." Rewrapping the snack, she glanced at the container of stew, open on the kitchen counter. "So, Caleb, were you just being polite when you invited me to dinner or does the offer still stand? I mean, I hate to rob you of Irene's great stew."

"There's plenty!" Minna said before her father had a chance to respond and before Gabby had a chance to ask herself what in heaven's name she was thinking. "And it's pretty good," Minna added. "For stew."

Turning to Cal, Gabby expected to see surprise, a little humor, maybe even a smidge of thanks-for-helping-out-with-the-prickly-preteen gratitude on his face. Instead, he appeared to be giving the matter a great deal of careful thought.

"Dad, you're, like, supposed to say something when someone asks if they can eat at your house."

Geez Louise. Gabby couldn't remember when she had so completely wanted to take back something she'd said. Because of some daft moment of kinship with these two solitary people, she'd set aside the caution she'd meant to exercise whenever Cal was around.

Wondering how to gracefully retract her request, she

stood about as comfortably as a manatee on dry ground until Cal emerged from his trance.

"That would be great," he said, his jaw stiff, as if he'd had it wired shut in the past two minutes. "We'd love to have you join us."

Sure you would.

What was his problem? Gabby wondered. *He* was the one who'd suggested dinner only minutes before in the dining room.

"On second thought," she said, turning apologetically to Minna, "I really should get home. I have about a gazillion things to do, and I'm trying to eat less red meat—"

A hand on her arm—warm, strong, beseeching—stilled her excuse.

"Stay." This time, Cal's request rode a tide of potent earnestness. "I want you to." When he realized he sounded like the King of Siam, he sighed and softened the request. "Please. I think my daughter and I both need a break from our own company."

For just a moment she got lost in his eyes, in their wry self-deprecation and in the way they searched hers. She had to consciously shake herself free from the spell he cast without even trying.

Getting involved with this family would only complicate her life, just when she was on the verge of figuring it out.

Better leave, her rational mind advised.

Stay with us, Cal's expression implored.

She stayed.

Chapter Six

"So Michaela Evans, who swears she can hold her breath underwater for two minutes, stands on the bottom of the lake with Kim Rutin standing on her shoulders."

"On Michaela's shoulders?" Minna asked Gabby for clarification as they leaned back in their chairs, stuffed to the gills with Irene Gould's excellent stew and too many Suzy Q's for comfort.

"Yes," Gabby confirmed. "They saw this trick in the original *Parent Trap* movie."

"With Hayley Mills," Minna interjected.

"Right." Gabby grinned. "You know your old movies."

"Classic TV, too."

"Cool. Anyway, Kim is standing on Michaela, which makes it appear that the water is only up to her waist. Then she tells Julia Rydecker, who had her hair cut in a cute Meg Ryan shag and refused to get it wet all summer, that the water is really shallow in that part of the lake and she should come on in. And Julia does, because there's this camp counselor she's crazy about giving a rowing lesson a little farther out on the lake."

"So, Julia fell in all the way?" Minna's hazel eyes widened with horror and guilty enjoyment.

"Exactly."

"What happened then?"

"Well, Julia had been lying to the counselors about her age all summer, telling everyone she was fourteen when we all knew her birthday wasn't until December. And she never went anywhere without makeup. So-o-o, Michaela pops up from the water and holds out a tube of lipstick she'd been holding the whole time she was underwater. And she says to Julia, 'Want to borrow my lip gloss? You could use a touch-up.' It was really mean."

"And really funny?"

"Hilarious."

Minna and Gabby dissolved into giggles over the dunking of The Perfect Girl, their female bonding progressing nicely.

No question about it: This kid of Cal's was a keeper. Smart, a little sassy like Cal said, but so sweetly hungry to belong somewhere that Gabby's heart felt like a pull-toy in Minna's hands.

"Who wants some real dessert?" Cal broke in above the laughter. "I've got a quart of mint chocolate chip in the freezer and chocolate syrup in the fridge."

"If I eat one more thing, you'll have to roll me to the door," Gabby declined, folding her napkin and setting it beside her dessert plate, where only the chocolate crumbs of a packaged cupcake remained.

"Just like Violet Beauregard in the original *Willy Wonka and the Chocolate Factory.* You know, the one with Gene Wilder." Minna grinned. "Remember when the Oompa Loompas had to roll Violet away?"

Grinning, Gabby complimented Cal. "Your daughter knows who Gene Wilder is. I love her."

"Chip off the old block." He winked at his daughter, who winked back. The earlier tension between them had evaporated, leaving Gabby with what she figured was a more accurate impression of their relationship: Cal and Minna were pals.

"Dad got me an *I Love Lucy* DVD collection," Minna announced proudly. "The entire first four seasons in a boxed set. You should come over for a Lucille Ball marathon!"

Gabby couldn't help it; she gaped at Cal with undiluted surprise. "Did you watch *I Love Lucy* when you were a kid?" she asked him.

He shook his head. "I discovered classic TV in college. Late nights with textbooks and *My Favorite Martian*."

"You and Ray Walston with antennae protruding from his scalp?" Gabby crowed with laughter. "I cannot picture it. I'd have figured you for a James Dean fan."

"Who's James Dean?" Minna asked, engrossed in the conversation.

"You don't know James Dean?" Gabby widened her eyes comically. "Your education is not yet complete, young lady."

"I'm saving Jimmy for her teenage years," Cal warned. "No point in rushing the moody discontent."

"Dad, I'm ready now."

Gabby laughed. "And on that parenting moment, I'm outta here."

"Thanks a lot," Cal grumbled. "You started it."

Grinning, she started to rise, surprised when Cal grasped her wrist.

"Seriously, stay," he requested, his gaze penetrating and as warm as the summer evening. "Friday is movie night at the Wellses'. I picked up the first Harry Potter. It's not a classic yet…."

"But it will be," she murmured.

I Love Lucy marathons, ice cream sundaes, movie nights… *Gabby, this is not the Cal you remember.*

She started to decline automatically. When her mother phoned her at work with the request that Gabby deliver food to Cal and his daughter, Gabby had tried hard to wriggle out of it, figuring the less contact she had with Cal, the less she would have to worry about old secrets. Plus, she hadn't thought it was possible to look at one's only lover in thirty-three years without feeling a whole lot of things she'd rather not feel, including, but not limited to, heated embarrassment.

And yet here she was, relaxed and enjoying herself, the first time in ages that she didn't feel the pressure to change—to sell the business, make her life more exciting, transform…change, change, change.

Despite his earlier James Dean-esque moodiness, Cal looked at her now with sincere invitation sparkling in his eyes.

Imagine, she thought, *Caleb Wells's eyes can sparkle without a hint of angst detectable.* What had he done with the troubled boy she remembered? It was tempting to stay and find out.

Not to mention that Gabby loved the Harry Potter books and figured she and Minna could spend a mighty pleasant evening trying to one-up each other with Hogwarts trivia.

She pictured herself on Cal's sofa, sitting next to Minna, probably indulging in those ice cream sundaes Cal had offered, with Cal dropping onto the sofa beside her.

That's when the Weird Thing happened.

Suddenly, in less time than it took for her heart to beat,

memory transported her to that night beneath the oak tree and the velvet, glittering Fourth of July sky. The night when Cal's body had been so close a feather could not have slipped between them. And she remembered how excited she had been—

"Gotta go!" she said, standing as if the dining room chair had bitten her on the rump, and forcing Cal to release her wrist at the same time. "I have some...business to take care of." Heavens, did it sound as if she was panting?

Cal checked his watch. "Seven-thirty Friday evening. It's officially the weekend. Can your business wait?"

Tell him, the voice of sanity urged. *Tell him that your "business" involves creating a more-than-flattering self-portrait on an internet dating site. Because right now she was picturing spending quality time with Caleb Wells instead of finding someone with whom to practice dating, and that wouldn't do. That wouldn't do at all. Maybe if she spoke out loud, it would alert her imagination that Cal was off-limits for what she had in mind.*

"I'm afraid not," was all she said, however, feeling small when Minna's face fell farther than her father's. "This has been great. Really. Especially getting to know you, Minna. I hope the second week of camp goes better than the first."

As Cal stood, Gabby edged toward the door. "Don't get up."

"Don't be silly." He followed her. "Min, you want to say goodbye?"

"Bye," the girl said without moving. She sounded somewhat dejected again, and Gabby hoped the mention of summer camp hadn't dragged down her mood.

Brows pulling together at his daughter's tone, Cal angled his head toward the foyer. "I'll walk you out."

When they reached the front door, she turned to say a final goodbye, but he followed her onto the porch and closed the door behind them.

"You should have kids."

Oh. Wow. That kind of choked her up, seeing as how she'd been dying to get married and make babies throughout her fertile twenties and had struggled mightily the past few years to come to terms with being childless.

"Thanks." She shrugged at Cal. "But I've kind of committed myself to being the favorite aunt. You know, the one who's incredibly fun when she's home then shoots off to exciting adventures and shows the kids how happy a woman can be on her own."

"You've thought this through."

"Yep."

"Well, your brother's children will certainly benefit. That was the happiest Minna's been all week." His gentle smile was half for her, half for Minna. "I owe you, Coombs."

The hot June day had mellowed to balmy yellow, breezeless and warm, and Cal stood far too close for comfort.

Say something. Gabby's tongue felt as if it were tied in a bow. "Mmnnn," was all she came up with.

Good enough for Cal, apparently. Leaning forward, placing a hand on her shoulder, he kissed her cheek— a soft, butter-smooth kiss that grazed the corner of her mouth and afforded a whiff of cologne and pheromones.

When he pulled back, his eyes looked more summer green than autumn hazel. "Thank you. Come back anytime, Gabby."

"Ahhehh." Not sure whether she meant *yes, definitely* or *not on your life, buster.*

Smiling at him—really just a small, short-lived jerk

of her stiff lips—she fled down the porch steps, wishing she'd brought her car so she could crank up the music and drown out her thoughts during the four blocks home.

Instead, she had to listen to her foolish head as it whispered terrifyingly, *What if you'd been Caleb's girl all along?*

Honey Bea's Bakery smelled like sugared heaven even after closing.

As Gabby, Lesley, Julie and Gabby's mother, Nancy, clustered around the long table used for kneading and shaping the luscious breads Honey Bea's turned out daily, Claire Kingsley, manager and lead baker, trotted out an array of cake samples for the women to try.

"I never baked wedding cakes before I came to work here," she confessed, setting out forks so each person could taste every flavor of cake. "Now wedding cakes are my favorite thing to create."

"You did a wonderful job with Dean and Rosemary's," Julie complimented. "Where did you learn to make sugar flowers?"

"Fletcher bought me a cake decorating class for Christmas. I stayed in Portland for a week and went to culinary school."

"Awww," the women chorused, struck by Fletcher's thoughtfulness. All except Gabby, who couldn't concentrate on anything today. This morning she'd nicked sweet old Mr. Guppy, who was on blood thinners, during his shave. Even with styptic powder, the poor man had bled for fifteen minutes.

Four days ago, Cal had kissed her on the cheek, and she'd been somewhat, well, actively thinking about sex with him ever since.

"Will you stop that?" Lesley leaned over to whisper in Gabby's ear.

Gabby removed her thumbnail from between her nibbling teeth. "Stop what?"

"Swinging your foot. You've kicked me three times. This is bothering you, isn't it?"

This was Julie's wedding cake tasting. The plans for her brother and future sister-in-law's wedding were rolling right along, thanks to a firm shove from Gabby's parents, who wanted to see wedding rings in place before the doctor told Julie to push.

It was true that the announcement of Dylan and Julie's nuptials had elicited a torrent of joy and self-pity inside Gabby. Another wedding. Another occasion to watch love weaving around two people as tangibly as if they were wrapping each other in Maypole ribbons. Another dateless reception.

Julie had asked Gabby and Lesley to be in her bridal party, offering the bride-to-be's obligatory refrain "...and I've chosen a gown that will look good on everyone," which as good as guaranteed the color teal and the presence of taffeta.

But none of that contributed to Gabby's current anxiety. Nope. Blame Friday night for that.

"I'm going to tell Mom I forgot to lock the back door to the shop," Gabby whispered to Lesley. "Offer to come with me."

"Okay."

Forks began slicing into feather-light cakes with distinctly luscious fillings, the cake tasting eliciting immediate *mmms* and *ahhs*.

"Oh, my gosh, I forgot to lock the door to the shop!" Gabby announced after she and Lesley had sampled three cakes each.

"Oh, my heavens!" her sister-in-law chimed in on cue. "I'll come with you."

"Hurry back," Julie said distractedly, obviously puzzled by her flavor options. "I want your opinions."

"For an October wedding, the white sponge with hazelnut mousse, no question," Lesley said, discreetly bringing her purse, aware the trip across the street might not involve a return to the bakery. "And for the groom's cake, the dark chocolate with Grand Marnier."

"You think so?" Julie asked Nancy, who nodded broadly. Claire grabbed a notepad and they began to work on the design as Gabby and Lesley left the bakery.

In the shop across the street, Les sat in one of the two barber chairs, using a pair of Gabby's scissors to trim her bangs. "Spill," she said to Gabby. "You looked like you were on a sugar high before you took the first bite of cake. Why are you so jittery? Have you gotten a response from the dating site?"

"Not yet." Gabby flopped into the second chair. "Unless you count the eighteen-year-old actor from Yemen who wants his green card and asked whether I know Vin Diesel."

"Could be promising."

Gabby watched tiny snips of Lesley's hair float to the floor. "Cal kissed me Friday night."

The scissors and Lesley's head jerked up at the same time. "Don't blurt that kind of thing when I'm holding something pointy! I nearly blinded myself." Her mouth opened in shock and delight. "Can we call off the internet hunt for a dance partner? Are you going to bring Cal to your first tango class?"

"No." Rising, Gabby took the scissors and began trimming Lesley's bangs. "He only sort of kissed me," she elaborated. "On the cheek. As a way of saying thank you for helping with his daughter."

"Oh." Disappointed, Lesley shrugged as Gabby worked. "Well, men do that. It doesn't necessarily mean anything, I suppose." She paused. "Unless, of course, you liked it." As Gabby's face turned red, Lesley's expression grew hopeful once more. "You did! You liked it a lo-ot," she sang.

"I'm in charge of your bangs, so don't annoy me," Gabby cautioned. Her confusion over her reaction to Cal's kiss had kept her tossing and turning and losing sleep for the past several nights. Yes, she'd liked it a lot. And she was hoping fervently that liking it didn't mean anything.

"I think I'm just ready for a relationship, you know?" she reasoned aloud to Les. "I think this is simply a good indication that I'm over Dean and ready to start having real relationships instead of fantasy relationships. I don't think my reaction was actually about Cal at all."

She looked at Lesley for confirmation that her reasoning was sound. Her sister-in-law offered a lightly arched brow. "Uh-huh. How did you help with his daughter?"

Finished with cutting Lesley's bangs, Gabby used a comb to sweep them over her forehead in a side part. "Minna's having a rocky time settling in. I hung out with them a little and talked to her about Camp Buford. Told her some stories about when we went there."

"Cal's daughter is at the camp?"

"Yes, but Cal thinks she's not enjoying it."

"Kate's gone to Burpford the past two summers. Maybe we can introduce them."

"That'd be nice. I think it goes beyond not knowing people, though. Minna has cerebral palsy. She feels self-conscious."

Lesley's expression turned sympathetic. "Plus she's new

in town, and Mother-Daughter Day was just announced. Do you think her mother will be able to attend?"

"Cal's ex is living in Europe. What's Mother-Daughter Day? I don't remember that."

"The camp started it a few years ago. Takes place in August. The moms spend a day participating in all the camp activities and the girls bake scones and serve the tea."

"I wonder if that's what's bugging her. If it is, I bet she hasn't told Cal about it. He seemed confused by her attitude toward camp."

"Poor guy. It's hard enough to understand a preteen girl, but when you factor in divorce, a long-distance mom, a move across the country and physical challenges…" Lesley wagged her head. "Cal must have his hands full." They were silently thoughtful then Lesley suggested, "Maybe someone should give Cal a heads-up about Mother-Daughter Day."

Gabby was thinking the same thing, but noticed the extra glint in her sister-in-law's eye. Quietly, she reminded, "I'm leaving in two months. It wouldn't be fair to connect with Minna and then disappear."

Les considered her carefully. "It wouldn't be fair to connect with Minna, or it wouldn't be fair to connect with Minna's dad?"

Setting down her scissors and comb, Gabby began to clean up around Lesley. "There's no reason to assume Cal is even interested—and neither am I—so that's all a moot point."

"Then why did you tell me about the kiss in the first place?"

"So I could forget it. Like with a bad dream. You tell it out loud to somebody else and then it doesn't come back."

"That never works."

Blowing out a huge puff of air, Gabby shook her head. "Come on. Let's go back to Honey Bea's and eat wedding cake samples. I'm obviously not going to get any help from you."

Gathering her purse, Lesley followed Gabby demurely out the back door. She didn't say another word until Gabby had locked up.

"Does Cal tango?" When Gabby glared at her, Lesley shrugged. "Just wondering." Then she started to chuckle.

Gabby sighed. "What?"

"Oh, nothing, nothing. It's just that being in Honey Comb's and hearing that you and Cal kissed made me think of a proverb Max told Eric when we were dating. Something about kissing being like salted water. You drink and your thirst increases." She smiled innocently at Gabby in the encroaching twilight. "I'm sure that doesn't apply to you, though. You have yourself firmly under control."

Chapter Seven

In their last two years of high school, Cal and Gabby had shared the same lunch period—11:30 to 12:20. On most days, Gabby brought her lunch (something dietetic) from home, purchased a drink in the cafeteria and was typically seated with her friends by 11:40.

All through junior year, Cal had shown up every day at 11:45, his lunch in a rolled-up bag—sometimes paper, sometimes plastic from the market—and asked in his sober, almost indifferent way whether there was room at Gabby's table. He could have sat without asking—there always was room—but no; every day, the same question: "Do you have room for one more?"

At first her friends had felt awkward around Cal, and he had rarely joined their conversation. Most everyone in school had been aware that he lived with his mother and aunt and, moreover, that both women had spent more time at local bars than at home. Cal had never been part of the "in" crowd, but by their third year of high school, he had managed to grow big and good-looking enough to garner interested looks and comments from even the most sought-after girls. Yet day after day he'd joined Gabby's small table of needy coeds, the ones who'd been too chubby or too shy or too intelligent or too damn something to be truly popular. Eventually, Cal's silence had seemed companionable, his presence expected and comfortably accepted...except by Gabby, who had started to feel certain *un*comfortable sensations, especially when she caught Cal looking at her.

Prior to their late teens, Cal had been more or less like another brother, though not nearly as annoying as the siblings with whom she'd grown up. Secretly, she had liked the fact that he was protective of her, his respectfulness a far cry and welcome respite from her brothers' incessant teasing.

Then they had turned seventeen and *zing-o.*

Suddenly, Cal's presence had begun to whip up a heat and confusion that had felt positively weird to Gabby. Then one day she had asked herself whether she was *attracted* to Caleb Wells, and a voice in her brain had answered positively, *No!* The sensation she had when she thought of Dean Kingsley—as if she were falling into a soft, *safe* pillow—*that* was the feeling she wanted.

Then there was that July Fourth night, the awkwardness after, the fact that before he'd left for college he'd hooked up with Grace Grassley from the varsity cheer squad....

All of that was on Gabby's mind as she walked up a flight of stairs that led to the small suite of offices above the Key Bank building on Main Street. According to her brother Ben, Cal had an office of his own up here.

Deliberately dressed down in the jeans and customary white blouse she wore to work, Gabby walked through the hallway, examining the doors for suite 206. When she found it—no nameplate yet, announcing Cal's presence—she raised a sweaty hand, curled her fingers into a fist and knocked.

Best to simply state her business, let him do whatever he wanted with the information she gave him and then go.

Gabby heard movement inside the office a moment before the door swung open, and his welcoming smile sent butterflies fluttering like crazy in her belly. "Gabby! This is a surprise."

"I know. Sorry. I'm sure you have to get to work. And, really, so do I—" She stopped talking when he reached out to grasp her wrist.

"It's a good surprise. Come on in."

Tugging her gently over the threshold, Cal shut the door and waited for her to explain the reason for her visit.

Finding speech easier without his touch, Gabby eased her arm away, smiling to show she was comfortable, very comfortable. "This is a roomy office," she commented, nervous about the topic she'd come to discuss. "You have two desks."

"One is for Minna."

Just as it had at Cal's house, Gabby's heart softened around the awareness that Cal was a loving and committed father. The potential to be a great dad had always been one of Dean's most attractive qualities—

Clearing her throat, she said, "Well, I'll get to the point."

Cal held a hand out toward one of the two chairs in the room. "Have a seat." He was dressed much more casually than before, in jeans and a T-shirt.

"I'm not going to stay long," she said, declining his offer to sit.

"I'm in no hurry. I don't start work officially until the

end of the month." Walking to the chair he'd positioned by the window overlooking Main Street, Cal seated himself while she stood, rather awkwardly, by the door. Leaning back, he crossed his arms behind his head and waited, a silent challenge to pry herself away from the door and sit down. More than ever, he resembled the boy she remembered.

"I've got to open the shop. Oh! That reminds me..." She dug into her pocket, withdrew a twenty-dollar bill and held it out. Cal didn't move, just rocked back on his heels, staring at her.

Gabby set the bill on a stack of boxes. "It's the money you left for the trim I didn't complete. I've been meaning to apologize about that, by the way. Although it looks as if you had it taken care of."

Backlit by streaks of morning sunshine, Cal nodded. "When I picked up Minna in Chicago."

Gabby nodded in return, wondering if she had any business being here at all this morning, when Cal rocked forward suddenly, startling her. He clasped his hands loosely, elbows on his knees.

"I've been wondering," he said, "where I'm going to get my hair cut now that I live here. You're the only barber for miles."

"There's Delilah at the Hair Hive. She works on men and women."

Cal smirked. "I don't mean to tell you your business, Gabrielle, but when it comes to haircuts there are two kinds of men. The kind who go to salons and the kind who go to barbers. I'm a barber man."

"There'll be a new barber here by September."

Sitting up straight, Cal ran a hand over his perfectly trimmed head. "Guess I'm going to be growing it out for a while."

He looked so boyish as he hinted that he wanted her to cut his hair, and Gabby felt that weird, uncomfortable pull low in her belly, as if her body paid no attention to anything her mind had decided.

"There are barbers in Bend," she said. "Ben goes to a woman he really likes."

"Your brother would like any barber he can flirt with."

"Well, that's true."

Finally accepting that she wasn't going to sit down, Cal rose, but remained near the window, haloed by the golden June morning. "Did you come here because you wanted to return the money?"

"No." *I came here to butt in.* "It's been a couple of days since I had dinner with you and Minna."

"Five."

"Is she still having a tough time?"

He sighed. "She's not happy."

Rubbing her palms on the rough denim covering her hips, Gabby hoped she was doing the right thing. "My niece is attending Camp Buford, and my sister-in-law mentioned something I thought you should know."

"All right." Cal's interest sharpened. "Shoot."

"Lesley told me the camp is hosting a Mother-Daughter Day. Has Minna mentioned it to you?"

Cal shook his head, his broad shoulders stiffening as he went on the alert. "Tell me about it."

"They didn't have it when I was a camper. According to Lesley, the mothers or other significant women in the girls' lives participate in a day of typical camp activities. Then the girls treat them to a tea. Sounds like fun...if you have someone to bring."

Cal rubbed his furrowed brow then shoved his fingers through his hair. "That's got to be what's bugging her.

She'd have told me about it, otherwise. This week she's barely spoken to me."

"The event doesn't happen until August. Is there any chance Minna's mother—"

Cal started shaking his head before Gabby finished. "Victoria is in Paris. She and Minna Skype once a week. Vic was never very hands-on when it came to parenting. Now she's working on a business project that consumes most of her time and attention. Also, there's a man involved."

Cal's tone gave no indication that he cared about the other man, but Gabby was intrigued. "Someone new?" she asked, watching carefully for his reaction.

"Her boss. Not new."

Her boss. Indignation curled Gabby's toes. Cal's ex-wife had cheated on him? And on their beautiful daughter? "That's unconscionable," she said, nauseous from the very thought of it. "I'm so, so sorry."

Taking several steps toward the middle of the room, Cal stopped short of reaching her. "How do you know I didn't cheat on my wife before she cheated on me?" he asked quietly.

This close up, the fine lines radiating from the corners of his eyes were visible. More important, Gabby could see what wasn't visible. Cal had always possessed a staunch integrity, a basic decency he demanded of himself.

Not a shade of uncertainty colored her voice. "You didn't."

Though his expression barely changed, Cal's body seemed to swell with feeling. Without her being aware of it, he must have taken another step or two toward her, because suddenly he was close enough to reach out and tuck one long, curly strand of red hair behind her ear.

"Still loyal," he murmured. "I wonder if Dean ever appreciated that?"

"I don't want to talk about Dean," Gabby choked, surprised Cal had even brought him up again. "Anymore." *Ever.* She was so tired of living her life mostly in her imagination that she couldn't stand even to think about it. In any case, she hadn't mooned after the man for years because she was *loyal.* She had done it because... Because...

Why?

Some awareness, some sharp, crystalline knowledge darted across the roads of thought winding through her brain. But the flash disappeared too quickly for her to examine it.

Her eyes refocused on Cal. He was staring at her, but his thoughts were shuttered.

It took a moment for her to realize that his hand had settled on her shoulder. Now she felt his fingers press into her skin.

Taking another step toward her, Cal seemed to block the light in the room with his big body. The space between them compressed—though she was sure *she* hadn't moved—and then Cal's lips were on hers.

Warm and smelling of aftershave, his skin was texturally perfect, not too rough, not too smooth. And the kiss itself...

Cal parted her mouth with his, but only a little— enough to leave no doubt that this kiss was more than merely friendly. His hands, so warm, so protective, came up to cup the sides of her face, and his lips moved with the softness of butterfly wings. No haste, no frantic agenda. There was only Cal, giving without a demand for anything in return.

Gabby stopped thinking. She felt like the flower from

which the butterfly drank, and even though they were indoors, sunshine spilled all around her. It was so incredibly sweet....

And then it was over. Cal stepped back.

Gabby kept her eyes closed. Her head whirled. She felt dizzy and wonderful and... Awkward. *What now?* Sanity returned too quickly, like a shock of cold water, and with it arrived the first stirrings of anxiety. Could she possibly back out of the room without acknowledging what just happened? Or looking at him?

"Gabby, open your eyes."

Apparently not.

Blinking, Gabby did as requested. Cal simply gazed down at her, in no apparent hurry to explain himself.

It took a more secure woman than she to be comfortable with the silent sexual tension—it was sexual on her end, at any rate—that stretched between them.

"Well." She cranked up her bright, we're-all-adults-here smile. "I need to open the shop."

"Wouldn't you like to talk first?" he murmured.

Stuffing her hands into the pockets of her jeans, Gabby shook her head. "No, not particularly. You know how some women love to talk about everything that happens to them?" She shook her head vigorously. "I'm not like that. Me, I'm perfectly comfortable with avoidance. Dodge and evade—that's me."

She continued to back up, and Cal watched her until she bumped into the door. Feeling behind her for the knob, she nodded her goodbye, making it halfway out before Cal spoke again.

"Gabby?"

"Hmm?"

"I'm not comfortable with avoidance." The planes

of his face were as solid as granite, but his eyes burned with expression. "Not anymore."

Cal leaned against the telephone pole on the corner of Fifth and Main. The camp bus dropped Minna off at four-thirty every weekday afternoon. She sat near the exit to circumvent a long walk up the aisle, and the driver carried her backpack to the door, where Cal swung her down so she wouldn't need to tackle the steps. Today he knew they needed to tackle a lot more than bus steps.

Mother-Daughter Day. That had to be contributing to Minna's foul mood over the past week. A good father would find a way to broach the topic so that his moody preteen would open up to him. Then that great dad would do something heroic, like put on a wig, show up at camp at the designated time, go swimming, ride a horse, drink tea and nod humbly when the "other" mothers told him how phenomenal he was.

He rubbed the bridge of his nose beneath his sunglasses and folded his arms over his chest. Being a phenomenal father took more skill, effort and ego reduction than anything Cal had ever done in his entire life. There were times when he'd have given an appendage or two if he could have picked up the phone and hashed out issues with Victoria. It wasn't that their divorce wasn't amicable; Vic simply didn't take much interest.

Cal had grown used to being a single parent even before his marriage ended. In fact, until Gabby joined him and Minna for dinner, he had grown so used to the stress that he'd failed to realize how isolated he felt. Gabby at the dinner table had turned an ordinary night into something that felt like family.

His first marriage, unsatisfying as it had been, had not

soured him on the institution. He'd always known that with the right person, marriage would fit him like a glove.

Cal sighed heavily and with great frustration. Behind his dark glasses he squinted as his head embarked on a dull throb that usually signaled an all-night headache.

When Gabby had first said she'd eat with them, he'd known he was jumping into choppy waters. That was why he'd hesitated. Minna had brightened and relaxed in Gabby's lively, accepting presence. Once his daughter met Gabby, she wanted more.

He could relate.

Midway through dinner, Cal had felt himself surrendering once again to the feelings she engendered—the warmth, the comfort, the challenge, the rightness. The pedestrian evening had proven what he'd always suspected: Gabby was his destiny.

Cal swore. Straightening away from the telephone pole, he tried to shake off any cloying sentimentality and to remind himself he was no longer a horny, needy teenager with a dog-eared copy of *Giant*. Cal still remembered the movie version of the book, with wrong-side-of-the-tracks James Dean longing for perfect and pure Elizabeth Taylor. In the movie, James had grown old alone and bitter, because Liz's heart had never been available to him.

By the end of the evening with Gabby, Cal had felt himself longing for her again. Hoping, despite every caution he gave himself, that he might have a future with the woman he had never been able to forget. Then this morning he'd dropped all notion of resisting and kissed her.

Same old Cal, wanting the moon when there were over two hundred thousand miles between him and it. Two hundred thousand miles of other life and space to be explored. What did he always tell Minna? "Envy is thin because it bites but never eats." That was a Spanish proverb Gabby's grandfather had shared with him. Better—far better—to enjoy what you've got than to brood about what you want, but can't have.

Two months. That's all he could have with Gabby before she left town, and that was only if she was willing. He couldn't tell after the kiss. Would two months be enough to get her out of his system once and for all?

In the distance, Cal saw Minna's bus rumbling lazily toward the Main-Fifth intersection and knew it was time to shift his brain away from the woman he never seemed to be able to forget and put his focus entirely on the one person who would always be with him. Like any good addict, however, he allowed himself one more thought: *What if Gabby is willing?*

"Min! Come on down, kiddo. Pizza's getting cold." Standing at the foot of the stairs, Cal waited for a response from his daughter, who had ignored his first two requests to join him for dinner and a cozy father-daughter tête-à-tête. "Minna!"

Silence.

He'd agreed to let her move upstairs without installing a chair lift, provided she got herself *carefully* downstairs on time for meals, and, when the time came, school. Where was she right now?

Antsy because he intended to broach the subject of Mother-Daughter Day over dinner, Cal took the steps two at a time and quickly arrived at his daughter's open bedroom door. Minna was at her desk, working on her computer, her back to her father.

"Min?" She'd been ignoring him, which made this one of those parenting moments when his head became a pressure cooker ready to blow.

"Dad, you've got to see this!" She spoke without turning around, her eyes glued to the computer screen.

"Min, I've been calling you—"

"Dad, that friend of yours—Gabby? She's on a dating site."

It took a couple of seconds for Minna's words to register. When they did, Cal flew to his daughter's side as if the movement were an involuntary response. "She is?" He bent to look at the monitor then realized, "Wait a minute, what are *you* doing on a dating site?"

Minna turned to look up at him, her beautiful eyes framed by thick, ink-black lashes and looking especially large as she blinked at him twice. "Dad, what do you think? I'm looking for you, of course." She pointed to the computer monitor. "You should post your profile on this site. There are a lot of local women on here and not many men. Your chances would be pretty good, I bet."

"They would, huh?" Cal scrubbed over his face. My God, this had been easier when she was four and all he'd had to worry about was whether the library had her favorite Barney video. "Look," he said, studiously avoiding a glance at the profile currently on the screen, "I don't know why you think I'd want this or why *you* want me to look online for a date, but—"

"Dad, it's pretty obvious. Mom's moved on, and you haven't gone on a date in *years* because of me."

"Min, because of you, I haven't *had* to go on meaningless dates. There's a difference."

"Right. It's more fun to worry about me than to go dancing."

Cal crouched down to go face-to-face with her. "Is this what's been bothering you lately? You think I want to ditch my best girl and go to a club?" He didn't miss the rolling of her eyes, but reached out anyway to tug a strand of silky black hair.

Did she have any idea how beautiful she was? The older she got, the more Cal's heart swelled with pride and protectiveness. The first boy who wanted to date his daughter was going to face a trial by fire from her father, no question.

"We used to dance," he murmured, smiling at her, "you and I. I'd turn on music, you'd put on your favorite princess outfit, then I'd lift you up and off we'd go." His smile filled his voice. "Sometimes we'd dance so much, my arms would shake, but every time I slowed down, you'd beg for more. Your giggle—that was my gasoline. It kept me going. It still does, Min."

Her head was down; she seemed to be staring at her lap, but Cal caught the whisper of a responding smile, however small.

"You can't dance with me anymore, Dad. I'm too big and…"

Cal tensed, waiting for the rest of that sentence, but she swallowed the word.

"What?" he pressed, knowing he needed to hear her thoughts even if his gut rolled when he wondered what she might say.

Minna shook her head.

Cal pressed some more. "Come on, Min, talk to—"

"Dad! You're turning into a helicopter pop. Stop hovering. Just stop it, okay? You need to just…get a life, so you won't worry about me all the time!"

"Look up 'parent' in the dictionary, Min. The definition is 'He who worries'."

"It is not."

"Well, it should be." He reached for her hand. "Baby, I know you're not happy here, but there's always an adjustment period when you move." Remembering that parenting was nine-tenths straight courage, he broached the topic most on his mind. "I heard there's going to be a Mother-Daughter Day at your camp, and—"

Abruptly, Minna pulled away. Reaching for the crutch she'd set against the desk, she struggled to rise.

"No, listen." Cal redoubled his efforts. "I was thinking maybe I could come. You know, participate in all the camp activities and then—"

"No! Oh, my God, are you kidding?" Making it to her feet, Minna spoke without trying to turn around. "Dad, I'm different. I get it, okay? But I don't want to advertise it."

"Min, you're only as different as—"

"Stop! I don't walk the same way everyone else does, I don't have a mother here, and…I don't *like* it here. I *hate* it! And I'm not going to pretend!"

Honoring their agreement to let her "run" out of a room at her own pace, Cal rose but did not follow—though every instinct he possessed made him want to scoop his daughter into his arms and tell her how damned wonderful she was.

His gut began to twist into several kinds of knots. He heard Minna make her way to the bathroom, shutting the door behind her, and wasn't sure whether he was being compassionate or cowardly as he decided to give her some time to calm down.

He slumped onto the desk chair and swore.

Not for the first time, Cal wanted to blame someone for the challenges Minna faced—cerebral palsy, divorced parents, absentee mother, incompetent father. But blaming implied there was something wrong with her, and, damn it, that wasn't true.

Helicopter pop. Was he really that bad?

Probably.

He raised his gaze to the computer monitor, where his ten-year-old daughter had been exploring dating services on his behalf. A color photo of Gabrielle smiled—shyly, he thought—back at him.

Cal swore again. His daughter hated her life, and Gabby had posted her photo on a dating site. The world was going crazy.

Peering at the monitor, Cal checked the date beneath her picture and discovered that "Gotta Dance from the Pacific Northwest" had updated her page only a couple of days ago.

"She's leaving in two months!" he growled. "What the hell?"

Grabbing the mouse, he scrolled down. Gabby's photograph appeared recent, taken at a party of some kind. With her hair twisted up and a red halter dress showing off her shoulders, she smiled winsomely at the camera.

Why was she looking for a boyfriend now? And why on the internet?

Clicking a couple of different tabs, he tried to view more of her profile, but quickly realized he had to join the dating site to gain access to the information.

Closing the page, he shoved the mouse aside and abruptly stood, knocking over the desk chair. Righting it, he plunked the legs down hard on the carpeted floor. So Gabby was trying to "connect with other singles" on the web. Fine. It wasn't his right to judge. If she wanted to start a meaningless, time-limited fling with a total stranger only two months before she moved her address to the Pacific Ocean, what the hell. It wasn't any of his business at all.

Stomping to the hallway, Cal stood, irresolute, trying to decide whether he wanted to order his daughter down to dinner. Moodiness and possibly tears were sure to result.

Plowing his fingers into his hair, he rubbed hard. Females. If he couldn't figure out a little one like his daughter, how the hell was he going to handle Gabby?

Chapter Eight

She was matched!

The dating site Gabby had come to think of as a waste of time and money had actually come through.

"*HAP*-py To Dance With You in The Pacific Northwest" had responded to her profile:

"I enjoy dancing, wouldn't mind a few lessons. "Casual dating" fine as well. Perhaps a movie night? Will try not to step on your toes, figuratively or literally. If you're interested, we can meet on neutral ground...."

He'd signed his note "Hap."

Hap sounded too good to be true. After a quick confer with Lesley, whose advice had been "Text him now, before someone else gets him," Gabby had set up their first meeting for Saturday at 6:00 p.m., early enough to leave before dinner if Hap turned out to be older than her father, had a visa about to expire or evidenced any sign of multiple personalities. After only two weeks on Make Me A Match, Gabby knew what to beware of.

Seated in a booth at Tavern on The Highway—near enough to Honeyford for her to feel grounded, but not so close that they'd run into people she knew coming and going—Gabby fiddled with a bowl of pretzels already on the table when she arrived, then pushed them aside and clasped her nervous hands to prevent further fidgeting.

Hap had sent a great photo, his smiling face friendly and handsome, but not so gorgeous you had to wonder why he couldn't get a date. She had asked for his full name, but he had texted back to her, "I'm just Hap."

Cute. Hap and Gab. Gab and Hap. Not that this was going to turn into anything *permanent,* but it would be nice to spend the next couple of months getting her dating feet wet with someone fun and lighthearted. Shallow as it made her feel, she wouldn't mind having a date to her brother's wedding, either.

Glancing down, she tugged at the gold halter dress Lesley had helped her pick out. "Casual, sexy and perfect for dancing," her sister-in-law had said approvingly. Gabby thought the dress was tight and worried that the halter top might be a tad too revealing, but she'd surrendered the final word on wardrobe to her sister-in-law.

Smoothing the swirly skirt over her knees, she jumped slightly when a masculine voice inquired, "Gotta Dance?"

Gabby took a breath, filling her lungs with soothing oxygen and sending it through her system. "Yes." She looked up with a bright smile. "And you must be Hap—"

A tall, perfect Mount Rushmore of a man, with the timeless kind of face that deserved memorializing, gazed down at her. He was dressed for a date.

Only the fact that he'd referred to her as "Gotta Dance," her Make a Match alias, clued her in to the fact that he was, indeed, answering her internet ad.

"May I sit down, Gabby?"

Slowly, she shook her head. "You didn't."

Cal held up a hand. "I'm not stalking you. Let me explain—"

"Hap. You said your name was Hap."

"No, I didn't. I wrote 'Happy to Dance.'"

"'I'm just Hap,'" she reminded him through gritted teeth. "That's what you texted me."

"I didn't think you'd take me seriously. Hap isn't a name."

"Yes, it is. In *Death of A Salesman,* the younger brother's name is Hap. As if you didn't know." He had aced AP English.

Cal slipped into the booth, opposite her. He set a square, wrapped package on the table and leaned forward. "Give me a moment to explain. If you want me to leave after I've had my say, I'll go. Deal?"

"I want a drink."

"Sure. What'll you have?"

Under the circumstances, a large chocolate malt sounded good, but the Tavern served only alcohol and water. "Piña colada," she told the waitress Cal flagged over.

She was still dateless. The moment she got home tonight, she was going to send Make Me A Match a scathing note then finish packing for the cruise.

"You sent a photo," she reminded Cal. "A photo of someone who is not you."

"True. I know him, though. We roomed together during grad school. Nice guy. Married now. Four kids. Minivan."

Gabby picked up a pretzel and chucked it at his head.

Cal caught it. "You have every right to be angry, but you must be curious about how I came across your profile."

Sitting back against the booth, she folded her arms

across her chest. Cal's gaze dropped to her cleavage…
and remained there.

Heat trickled through Gabby's veins. It was an ice-
melting, summer's-coming, warm-you-to-your-toes kind
of heat. She sat absolutely still, and Cal… Well. He
couldn't seem to lift his eyes above her halter top.

"Okay," she admitted, clearing her throat when her
voice emerged like a croak, "tell me how you saw my profile." She narrowed her eyes, forcing herself to get tough.
"And then explain why you sent a fake response and why
I'm sitting across from you tonight instead of a real live
date."

"So your daughter's been scrounging dates for you."

Cal was glad to see that his explanation softened
Gabby's resistance to the fact that he was her date for the
evening. Stirring her melting piña colada with two skinny
red straws, she smiled at him.

Her whole face glowed when her lips curved. And
that dress she was wearing…it looked as if an artist had
painted the gold material on her, then sprayed the same
color in a dusting of freckles over her skin. He liked it. A
lot.

"And you registered for the dating service to appease
her?" Gabby continued. "That seems to be going above
and beyond the call of parenthood."

"I suppose," he murmured. Swirling his scotch, Cal
didn't bother to correct Gabby's impression. In fact, he'd
registered for the dating service solely for the purpose of
viewing her profile. Despite his logical self-talk, he hadn't
been able to stop thinking about it.

"Minna finally admitted she's afraid that I don't date
because of her."

"Is that the truth?"

"No!" He sipped his drink, which went down more sharply than it usually did. Divulging personal information had never been his strong suit, which no doubt accounted for the fact that he'd married a woman with whom he'd rarely been able to scratch the surface of any conversation. He was trying to do better with his daughter, but perhaps he was kidding himself. If he couldn't speak honestly to another adult, how was he going to model openness for his child? Gabby's grandfather was the only person in whom he'd ever confided, so now he admitted, "I'm a disaster at dating, Gabby. The subtleties of being intimate are…" He wagged his head ruefully. "…beyond me."

There. He'd said it.

With the words out, Cal exhaled heavily, not sure whether he was relieved or sorry that he'd spoken.

Gabby's beautiful red brows drew together. "Do you mean emotionally intimate or physically intimate or both?"

That question drew a genuine laugh. "No, I think I'm pretty good at the physical part." Heat suffused her face, which, he had to admit, was damn cute. He'd acquired a good bit of practical knowledge about making love since his one-night encounter with Gabby. Well aware their experience together had been her first and that he hadn't been able to give her the pleasure he'd wanted to, Cal would have been happy to show her how much he'd learned over the years if he could be sure that having sex wouldn't dramatically complicate their lives (it would).

Gabby was looking down, twirling a pretzel stick on her napkin. She looked beautiful. And troubled. Cal had a collection of unanswered questions about this woman.

Who had loved her in the years he'd been gone? What had the men been like? Why hadn't any of them stuck?

Somehow, like him, she had ended up single and still searching for a connection to end the loneliness.

"Talking about things that matter is more difficult than having sex, don't you think?" he asked softly.

The startled, aching look in her eyes shot an arrow of kinship straight to his heart, and suddenly he felt sure: Neither of them had figured out this thing called love.

Though Tavern on the Highway was filling with people, Gabby felt suddenly as if she were alone with Cal. The jukebox and symphony of conversation around them faded to keen silence.

She hadn't experienced physical intimacy since Cal or emotional intimacy with any man. Was one more difficult than the other? She couldn't say; for her, both had been as elusive as purchasing a winning lottery ticket.

Unsure of how to answer Cal's question, Gabby let her gaze wander to the dance floor, where couples two-stepped to a country song she'd never heard before. The lyrics seemed to pay homage to the singer's faithful dog and to justify his decision to spend Saturday with the canine rather than with a woman. The dancers grinned as they moved and one couple in particular appeared to be having a wonderful time.

Trying a double turn, a heavily pregnant woman laughed in delight as she navigated the move without bumping her stomach into her partner. Joy seemed to create a glow around her.

A sharp pang made Gabby hunch her shoulders. Her gaze slid to the man who was clearly enjoying the dance as much as the woman, and the pang became a pierce.

Dean.

"He hasn't changed much." Cal spoke from across the table.

The song ended with a musical flourish the dancers tried to emulate, and Dean put his arm protectively against his wife's expanded waist as she caught her breath. Whether by coincidence or because they felt interested eyes upon them, the couple looked straight at Gabby and Cal.

Rosemary recognized Gabby first and nudged her husband, who smiled broadly. King's Pharmacy was only a few doors down from the barbershop. Dean and Gabby used to be on the Chamber of Commerce together, and Gabby had been a frequent customer at the pharmacy. Thankfully, she'd stopped stalking Dean the day she'd realized he and Honeyford's new librarian were a hot item. Avoidance had then become her modus operandi, and she hadn't seen them more than a handful of times since the wedding.

"Smile or stop staring," Cal advised, his tone wry. "And take a breath before you pass out. They're heading over."

"I am not going to pass out," Gabby protested, resenting the insinuation. "And I wasn't staring. I was surprised to see someone so pregnant dancing, and then I realized—" She stopped when Cal's brow hitched. "Oh, never mind. I don't have to explain myself," she muttered decisively, eating one of the pretzels she'd been stockpiling on her cocktail napkin.

"Good," Cal approved. "I like you better angry than pitiful."

"I'm not pitiful." She slapped the pretzel onto the table. "I haven't been pitiful for weeks."

"Might want to take a show of hands on that." Inclining his head slightly toward the couple that approached the table, Cal murmured, "Time to grin and bear it, Coombs."

"Gabby, it's so good to see you!" Reaching their table, Rosemary Jeffers Kingsley beamed with the genuine grace characteristic of her. "I've been meaning to poke my head in the barbershop to say hello, but the library is so busy during the summer."

Smiling at the couple, who stood with their hands comfortably clasped, Gabby was unwilling to make a similar claim about visiting Rosemary. She had been avoiding the library for months, and figured Rosemary knew why. The sensitive woman had read Gabby easily and accurately at her wedding reception, assessing Gabby as suffering from unrequited love. The compassion in Rosemary's eyes had been more painful than resentment would have been.

Rosemary turned to Cal when Gabby numbly failed to speak. "I think we met at Honey Bea's. I'm Rosemary Kingsley."

Sliding from the booth, Cal rose. "I remember. A pleasure to see you again." Then he shifted his attention to the other man and extended his hand. "Congratulations."

The smile Gabby had once adored creased Dean's face handsomely. "Thank you." Firmly, he shook the proffered hand. "Caleb, isn't it? You used to come to the soda fountain with Gabby."

"Good memory."

"I haven't seen you in quite a while."

"I lived out of state for several years."

"Are you back for good now?" Rosemary divided her glance between Cal and Gabby. She looked hopeful.

"That's the plan." Changing the subject, he asked, "Do you two come here often?"

"It's where we first met." Dean grinned, just a fool in love with his wife. "We decided to stop in one more time before the baby comes."

A brief, slightly awkward silence followed, broken by Rosemary. "Gabby, you look lovely tonight. That color is fabulous on you. I wish I could wear it. Doesn't she look beautiful, Dean?"

Dean, who was still gazing at his gorgeous bride, reacted as if he'd had an elbow jabbed into his side. "Yes. You do look lovely, Gabby."

Oh, the humiliation! Traitorous heat filled Gabby's cheeks. She forcibly smiled her thanks for the forcibly offered compliment, but couldn't dredge up a word.

Resuming his seat, Cal reached for her fingers as they worried the edge of the cocktail napkin. "Gold is my favorite color on her. Although I'm biased. I think she looks good in everything." His smile was warm, caressing and suggestive.

Time stopped. The air in the room ceased moving. Gabby stared at Cal. He gazed back as if he'd forgotten they had company.

She frowned back at him. *Huh?*

"I think we've overstayed our welcome," Rosemary warbled as if she couldn't be happier by the turn of events.

Instead of correcting the impression that he and Gabby were a couple, Cal shrugged apologetically. "Sorry. You know how it is."

After a fair bit of grinning and the suggestion that they should all get together soon, the other couple left.

Gabby stared at Cal. "What do you think you're doing?"

"Saving your a—" he began then amended as the waitress stopped by to drop off a bowl of peanuts, "—face. We're on a date. It was my duty."

"We're not on a date."

"You're welcome."

His steady gaze and pointed smile stopped her. All right, she was grateful. At the very least, he'd saved her from Rosemary's pity. "Thank you. But you realize this will be all over town soon."

"That could work for us."

Realizing her fingers were still captured by his, Gabby attempted to tug free, but Cal refused to let go. "What are you talking about?"

"You haven't asked *why* I responded to your profile."

Gabby frowned. "For Minna."

With his free hand, Cal brushed the easy answer away. "I could have responded to ten other women if all I'd wanted was to placate my daughter. I wrote to you because you and I need the same thing."

Gabby's misbehaved fingers twitched beneath his. "What's that?"

"A favor."

Warily, she waited for him to elaborate.

"You're looking for a dance partner and occasional date, am I correct?"

"Desperately seeking," she quipped, though in light of the men who had so far applied for the position, it didn't seem so funny.

"And I want someone to attend Mother-Daughter Day with Minna."

"You're saying you want to do a trade?"

"That's right. I need a woman I can trust."

Slowly, Gabby shook her head, although her heart began to pound from a shot of straight adrenaline. *He's not asking you to go to bed with him; the man needs a favor for his daughter.* "Won't that be confusing for Minna? I'm leaving in two months."

"Which makes it perfect. You and I began as friends, and we'll end as friends. As for what happens in between…" He shrugged. "People date. They break up. It's part of life. Minna will understand that, and we'll all get what we want in the meantime."

Gabby took a moment to ponder this twist on her original plan. "So what I get out of the deal is a dance partner."

"A partner with rhythm and the decency not to maul you on the dance floor."

"Maybe I was looking for someone to do a little mauling."

He shrugged again. "Okay, I'll maul you."

Suddenly, Gabby's fingers sizzled like dough hitting hot oil. Once more she tugged her hand from his. This time he let her, folding his arms across his chest.

"We can keep this totally friendly, Gabby," he told her, speaking so quietly she had to lean forward. "Or we can rewrite our last encounter. Amend it from two teenagers experimenting with sex to two adults spending a couple of months showing each other what they've learned." Then he leaned back and smiled. "You choose."

Chapter Nine

Daylight savings time made it difficult to skulk on a summer evening, but Gabby did her best as she approached Delilah's—formerly Helen's—Hair Hive on Main and Fourth. Delilah was turning out the most progressive styles Honeyford had ever seen, and in the past year and a half, Gabby had lost a number of her regular clients to the other woman.

Gutting the salon's interior when she'd purchased it from the original owner, Delilah had turned her modest storefront into a high-end salon that served mimosas or wine while clients "processed," eschewed sponge rollers and spiral perms, and promised a "spa-like experience." Delilah, who was from California and, rumor had it, had been involved in the film industry, was a popular topic of conversation and sought after as a stylist, but she had not yet become a "local." In fact, Gabby knew not a single person in town who claimed to socialize with the sophisticated woman. Sleek, confident and aloof, she kept to herself. And she intimidated the hell out of Gabby, who had not stepped foot in the salon or, to her shame, made any attempt so far to welcome the other woman to town.

"'No one can make you feel inferior without your consent.' Eleanor Roosevelt," Gabby encouraged herself as she came abreast of The Hive.

Unfortunately, she gave her consent too damn often. Take, for example, last night.

"Then what did you say to him?" Lesley had asked her when Gabby phoned from her car on the way home from Tavern on the Highway.

Shocked and highly amused that Gabby's big date had turned out to be Caleb Wells, Lesley had climbed from bed, where she and the family had been watching reruns of *Wipe Out,* and had taken the cordless phone into her closet so she could grill Gabby to her heart's content.

"I laughed," Gabby had admitted, cringing at her sister-in-law's outrage.

"You laughed after a man suggested becoming lovers? Were you *trying* to verbally castrate him?"

"No, of course not! I panicked," Gabby confessed. "I wasn't positive he was serious, so I acted like I knew he was joking. That way, no one had to be embarrassed."

There was a considerable pause. "How'd that work for you?"

"Also," Gabby added, "I don't want to have sex with Cal."

"Of course not," Lesley scoffed. "He's real."

"I want real," Gabby insisted. "The men on the cruise will be real, too. But I'd rather wait. There would be far too many complications with Cal...assuming he is serious."

"Right, too many complications. Cal could, for instance, remember your name afterward. He might even care about you."

Gabby was momentarily too startled to speak. "What are you talking about, Les? I want someone to care about me."

"Gabby...pumpkin...I've known you most of my life. I'm sitting in the closet in my pajamas, and I'm missing *Wipe Out,* so I'm going to assume I have the right to speak frankly. Real relationships *are* complicated and messy, and sometimes they make you feel stupid. You want to get it perfectly right the very first time, but honey, you haven't even gotten your feet wet yet. You're going to make mistakes—it's inevitable. Cal is handsome as sin, he wants to make love to you, he's willing to take this one day at a time and not incidentally he has very nice table manners. Why don't you finish what you started with him? Make him your first lover, knowing that it's time-limited. Do you trust him to walk away nicely at the end of two months?"

"Yes."

"And I know you trust yourself to walk away."

"Right."

"Sounds perfect, then. You do find him attractive, don't you?"

Holy biceps, yes, she found him attractive. Her physical response to Cal trumped her response to Dean—or, quite frankly, anyone else—hands down. When he had grabbed her hand in front of Dean and Rosemary at the Tavern, Gabby had gone temporarily blind with desire—and not the desire for another woman's husband.

Seeing Rosemary all plump and glowing with pregnancy had thrown her for a loop, yes. But she felt the same treacherous shot of envy any time she saw a woman her age starting a family. Her physical response to Cal was stronger than anything she'd ever felt for Dean. Cal had misunderstood, and she hadn't corrected him, because...

"Because it's easier that way," she admitted, muttering to herself as she glanced around Main Street to see if anyone she knew was hanging about and might see her entering Delilah's Hair Hive.

For as long as Gabby could remember, she'd felt awkward about her femininity, fretting predominantly that she didn't possess enough of it. Four brothers and life on a farm hadn't set her up to become prom queen, and being the fat girl most of her youth had done little to enhance her self-image.

Last night, after speaking to Lesley, she had finally stared at herself in the mirror and admitted the truth: Dean never had been real to her. He'd never challenged her, never had a strong opinion about her, never loved her. She'd never run the risk of disappointing him.

She'd never yearned to have him rip her clothes off, either. Her former fantasies about Dean seemed rather subdued when she compared them to her thoughts about Cal.

Peering into the window of the Hair Hive, Gabby saw a styling station with tiny lights surrounding a mirror, like twinkling diamonds. She swallowed. Would Delilah's skill as a stylist help her feel more confident?

One of the other things Gabby had admitted to herself last night was that she'd been physically attracted to Cal in high school.

Of course you don't want to have sex with Cal, Lesley had accused her. *He's real.*

So real that he'd scared the heck out of her even then.

According to the sign in Delilah's front window, there were fifty-three minutes left until closing.

Gabby put her hand on the door handle. Just how nuts

was it to believe that a new hairstyle could bestow the courage she needed to start living in the real world?

A tap on the window startled her.

"Are you coming in or not?" Voice muted by the glass, a slender brunette cocked her head at Gabby. Her silver earrings caught the waning sunlight. "I take walk-ins, but I'm off in an hour, so if there's something you want, we should get started."

Gabby took a breath. Nuts or not, she opened the door.

"Don't open your eyes," Delilah warned as Gabby's lids fluttered.

Smelling of Joy perfume, the gorgeous hairstylist leaned over her customer, brushing eye shadow carefully along Gabby's brow bone. "The important thing is not to be afraid of color," she said in the throaty voice Gabby found rather hypnotic. "Redheads tend to shy away from the full color palette, but why rob yourself? If the tones are dusky, you can experiment with a variety of hues. Play," she encouraged. "The secret to makeup is to have fun. It's the secret to everything important, don't you think?"

"No question," Gabby murmured as the small makeup brush swept gently over her skin.

Delilah certainly looked as if she had fun. Dressed in a black off-the-shoulder, peasant-style top belted over skin-tight jeans, she'd accessorized her outfit with long strands of onyx beads and chunky black bangles. Delilah screamed "sex appeal." Gabby could easily imagine men falling over their own tongues to get near her. If the clever beauty expert couldn't get Gabby romance ready then nobody could.

After washing and cutting Gabby's red curls, Delilah had embarked on a makeup application lesson.

Brushing a second coat of lash thickening mascara—

"thickening for day, lengthening for night"—onto Gabby's naturally auburn lashes, Delilah addressed her client's lips then turned Gabby away from the mirror before she could get a look at herself.

"Wait for it. You want the total effect."

While Delilah ministered to Gabby's curls, Gabby looked around the small but chic salon. Instead of black-and-white photos of Honeyford's earlier halcyon days, Delilah had hung framed prints in bold colors to compliment her pumpkin-colored walls. One large picture, however, stood out as different from the rest.

A large color photo showed a lovely young girl wearing a huge grin and a pageant sash. "'Miss You Can Do It,'" Gabby read the words that danced along the bottom of the picture. "What is that?"

Wielding a curling iron through Gabby's red curls, Delilah took her time responding. "It's a pageant."

"A children's beauty pageant?"

"A pageant for girls with physical challenges."

Gabby widened her eyes and leaned forward. "No kidding?"

Delilah pressed her back in the chair. "No kidding," she murmured.

"Were you a stylist on staff?"

"Something like that."

The timeliness of this discovery was not lost on Gabby. A pageant for girls with disabilities could be a wonderful boon for Minna. "Tell me about it," she urged the salon owner.

Setting the curling iron aside, Delilah reached for a tube and squeezed some kind of cream onto her palm. "There's a website where you can get more information. Google it."

Delilah plunged her hands into Gabby's hair, fluffing

the roots, twisting a curl here and there. Gabby wanted to ask another question about the pageant, but Delilah swiveled the chair to the mirror at last. "You're done." Stepping aside, she allowed Gabby an unimpeded view.

"Holy cow," Gabby breathed.

Delilah laughed. "I take it you're pleased?"

Gabby nodded. *Pleased* was a pale understatement. Russet curls, full and soft and alive, cascaded over her shoulders. Even resting perfectly still they seemed to possess movement, as if a wind machine was blowing them. Gabby's complexion glowed like a summer peach, and her gray eyes stared in wonder, surprised by their own transformation from barely-there to smoky and come-hither. And the moist sheen on her parted lips…they begged to be kissed.

"You've got to come on the cruise with me," she told Delilah, only half-kidding. "I'll never be able to recreate this on my own." She pointed at the mirror. "That woman could get a date."

Removing Gabby's cape, Delilah wagged her head. "You're too funny. You make it sound as if seducing a man is difficult."

"Uh…yeah."

Delilah waved a well-manicured hand. "It's the easiest thing in the world. Being seduced is simply a superficial reaction to visual stimulus plus the willingness to lose control. Men are almost always willing to lose control."

That was either the most cynical or most brilliant dating tip Gabby had ever received. "May I quote you?" she asked.

Watching Delilah drop combs into disinfectant and replace caps on the products that lined up like good soldiers at her workstation, Gabby felt a mix of awe and envy. The most mundane task looked sexy as all get out when Deli-

lah performed it. Was that kind of appeal natural or culti-
vated? And why did some people receive so much natural
allure when others had to mine for it?

They spent the next quarter hour reviewing Gabby's
hair and makeup instructions. While Delilah loaded products into a glossy handled bag, Gabby's eyes strayed once
more to the Miss You Can Do It poster. The girl in the
photo seemed familiar, perhaps because Gabby could so
easily envision Minna on that poster. Minna was beautiful, but would she grow up without feeling it?

"Is Miss You Can Do It a national pageant?" she asked,
surprised when Delilah stopped what she was doing and
exhaled the way Lesley did when she taught yoga and
suggested that everyone "breathe out the stress."

"I put that poster up the day I moved in here," Delilah
muttered. "No one has ever asked me about it. Most people are only concerned with what they see in the mirror."
She looked at Gabby, her sad smile making her appear at
once elegant and older.

And lonely, Gabby thought. *She's gorgeous and sexy
and lonely.*

Curious and empathetic, Gabby slowly shook her head.
"Who is the girl in the photo?"

Delilah's gaze strayed to the poster in question. She
took a deep breath, letting it out slowly, attention becoming so focused on the photo that she seemed to forget she
had company. Though her large eyes remained dry, their
grief could have melted stone. When she spoke, her voice
was so soft, Gabby strained to hear the aching words. "My
daughter."

*The Waltz: Originally a folk dance, the waltz is smooth
and graceful, in triple time....*
The waltz was a safe choice for Gabby's first dance les-

son with Caleb. Or it had seemed like a safe choice until she rushed into the community center late on Thursday evening after visiting with her father, who was scheduled to have surgery in two days.

She'd stopped at home to don the skirt Lesley had instructed her to wear for dance class, to touch up her curls and to apply eye shadow, mascara—lengthening for nighttime—and lip gloss.

Cal was already present, chatting with Lesley when Gabby arrived. His expression altered the moment he saw her. The meaning behind his low whistle was unmistakable. "You're stunning."

Gabby ran a hand over the front of her ivory and turquoise skirt. *Stunning.* Her parents had offered a similar opinion, but Cal's reaction engendered a whole different response inside her. As he approached, the look in his eyes hugged her like a magnet. When he stood directly in front of her, his eyes made a leisurely tour of her face and the hair she'd moussed, scrunched and worn loose.

"Wow," he said, almost matter-of-factly.

"Makeover," she murmured. "Part of the new me."

"No. You always looked like this. The difference is that now *you* know it."

Oh. Wow.

Behind them, more students began filing into the oak-floored, multipurpose room. Two giggling teenage girls, a young couple in their twenties, a woman who came alone and looked nervous as could be, plus Irene Gould and a few minutes later, Henry Berns, who seemed surprised to see Irene. Henry brought a pink box filled with Honey Bunz to sustain them all and shared that taking ballroom dance classes had not been his idea; Claire thought it would be good for him and had signed him up. Gabby knew that Claire was trying to play matchmaker between

Henry and Irene. A glance at Irene's flushed face confirmed her suspicion that Irene had given her approval.

When Lesley announced the start of class, Cal held out a hand. "Ready to go?"

Gabby nodded. "Sure."

She clearly remembered her plea to Lesley two weeks prior: "Can we start with the waltz, please, and work our way toward the sexier dances?"

Now she took Cal's hand and felt every cell in her body wake up and sing. While Lesley counted, "One-two-three, two-two-three, three-two-three…," Cal moved them surely around the floor, his gaze steady on Gabby's face, and she stumbled more than once, which had nothing to do with learning the steps and everything to do with the fact that her blood actually felt hot as it coursed through her veins. Cal's hold tightened when she faltered, an encouraging smile curving his lips.

"We should have done this in high school," he murmured, "like them." He tilted his head toward the teenage girls, who continued to giggle as they tried to remember when to bend their knees and when to rise up on their toes. "They'll be pros by the time they're our age."

Gabby shook her head. "I couldn't have done this in high school."

"Why not? Dancing made you nervous?"

"Mmm," she said noncommittally as they step-together, step-together, step-together-ed around the room.

In high school, her attraction to Cal had scared the spit out of her, or it would have if she had ever acknowledged it. Fantasizing about Dean had been easier, as Lesley recently pointed out.

As they traced a box on the floor, Gabby realized she felt something other than excitement; she felt safety. In Cal's arms, it didn't matter that she stumbled or lacked rhythm, which, let's face it, she did. He held her with a tenderness that said he knew exactly who was in his arms.

After years of loving someone who hadn't loved her back, Gabby knew what invisible felt like. Now she was discovering how it felt to know a man truly saw her.

"Cal?"

"Hmm?"

"Just dancing wouldn't have made me nervous in high school. But I think dancing *with you* might have."

"You don't have to walk me home. This is Honeyford. It's still pretty darn safe around here."

Gabby stood with Cal outside the multipurpose room, deciding it would be best to beat a hasty exit before Lesley cornered her for a little grilling. "It's not even completely dark yet." In fact, the lavender sky gave the impression that evening had only just begun.

Beside her, Cal looked as if he fit into the summer night as naturally as stars fit into the heavens. Dark jeans and a leaf-green polo shirt covered his fit body, making him appear several years younger than he was. His glance traveled the near-empty street. "I've been in Chicago too long. I wouldn't let Minna go home by herself."

"I'm not ten."

"I know."

Cal took her arm and started walking.

"Where's Minna tonight?" Gabby asked.

"Remember Carolyn and Matt from high school? Their oldest daughter, Madeline, is babysitting at our place."

"Babysitting? Cal," Gabby admonished. "I may not have children, but I know that no self-respecting ten-year-old wants the term *babysitting* applied to her."

"Okay, Madeline is providing preteen care. Ten is too young to be home alone."

Gabby nodded, but she was amused. He sounded like her father—obstinate, protective and loving. With his fingers curved around her left elbow, Cal courteously walked beside her as they passed homes in which many of their friends had grown up. Some of those friends had moved to larger towns, some had stayed put to build their families right here in Honeyford.

Gabby got quiet.

"What's wrong?" Cal squeezed her elbow.

"My dad's having surgery in two days."

"I know. I spoke with him this morning."

"You did?"

"I call or drop by to check in every couple of days. I figure I have a lot of years to make up for." Cal glanced down. "Does that bother you?"

"No." It didn't. She was coming to understand that Cal had always had his own relationship with her parents. "I do still wonder how they'd react if they knew you and I…"

He waited a moment for her to complete the sentence, and she wanted to kick herself for feeling, at the ripe age of thirty-three, too vulnerable to use the term "made love" in regard to her and Cal. She could have said, "had sex," but that felt equally awkward.

When Cal was all through waiting for her to come up with an appropriate phrase, he said, "I'm not planning to tell them, Gabby. Not unless you've decided you want to." He raised a brow.

"No, I don't," she confirmed. "Especially not now, with Dad having surgery. His recovery will take a while, and he and my mother have a lot on their plates with Dylan's wedding and…my plans. I'm mostly concerned about my mom, I suppose. She's always seemed so in control, but this is a lot of change all at once."

They crossed B Street en route to the two-bedroom

bungalow Gabby had inherited from her grandfather. She didn't regret her decision to shake up her life by working for the cruise line, but with Dylan occupied, Eric busy with his family and Ben and Jeremy perennial bachelors who wouldn't know how to be caretakers if someone printed a manual on the palms of their hands, well...

"My mom tries to pretend she can do everything on her own," Gabby said, shuffling along next to Cal, "but she's not as resilient as she used to be. It's good to know you'll be nearby. I'm grateful you're in their lives again, Cal."

"They're family to me," he said immediately, then amended, "like family."

There were no paved sidewalks on Honeyford's side streets. Gravel crunched beneath Cal's and Gabby's feet. He'd let go of her elbow back on A Street. Now when she ceased walking, he paused, too. "Cal, there's something I've wondered for a long time. In fact, I've been meaning to ask you... Did you stop contacting my parents because of what happened between us?" That wasn't nearly specific enough, so she added, "I mean, because of the way I acted after that night?"

The sky was darkening now, lavender deepening to eggplant, and Gabby figured the cover of night was making her braver. She stopped and turned toward Cal. There were few street lamps to illumine his face, but she sensed his watchfulness.

"Why do you think I stopped coming over?" he asked, his deep voice hushed, no more than a brush of warm night air.

Gabby's throat felt dry as dust. This conversation had been a long time coming. Her apology was fifteen years late, but she owed it to him. "I avoided you the next day and most of that week. I can imagine how awkward that must have made you feel. And I'm truly sorry for how I behaved. I just felt so…foolish for throwing myself at you. And don't say that I didn't, because in all the years we knew each other you never came on to me. I was afraid you felt guilty when you realized how inexperienced I was and that you regretted the whole encounter." She took a deep breath and let it out. "I wanted to avoid the awkwardness between us, but by avoiding you, I created more discomfort. I'm sorry I ignored your attempts to talk to me. It was wrong."

The sound of Caleb's breathing, the crunch of gravel as he shifted and the squeaky melody of crickets warming up for the night were the only sounds Gabby heard for several moments.

Finally, he spoke. "I accept your apology. But aren't you forgetting something?"

She looked at him.

"Dean. He found his girlfriend at the river with Eli Stone just hours after introducing her to everybody as the future Mrs. Kingsley. They broke up the next day, and that opened the door for you and him again—which closed the door between you and anyone else."

"The door between Dean and me was never open."

"You didn't know that at the time, as I recall."

She nodded. "Okay, it's fair to say I thought I had a shot with Dean again, but that doesn't have anything to do with you and me."

With a snort of laughter, Cal turned and began walking again, quickly this time, on his way to Gabby's house whether she followed or not.

She trotted to catch up. "It didn't, Cal. I was wrong to avoid you, but you and I had no future, not in the romantic sense." As proof she offered, "You hooked up with Grace Grassley almost immediately."

"Did you care?"

"No, you didn't owe me anything! That's the point. I never should have put you in the position of feeling like you had to break off with me, or worrying about my reaction if you dated someone that summer."

Cal stopped dead. This time, the light from a front porch lit enough of his features for her to see that his expression was part disbelieving and part disgusted.

He looked at her a long time and then "Gabby," he said, shaking his head slowly, "you can be such a dummy."

Cal reached out, and his warm hands cupped her face. He stepped closer. Gabby felt her heart thud heavily in her chest. She could hear her own breathing.

How strange, she thought dazedly. The closer his face got, the more she felt she could see all of him—all the strength and passion and resolution that was Cal.

At the moment he seemed resolutely determined to kiss her, and she was resolutely determined to let him. The desire to touch him eclipsed every ounce of sense she possessed.

Time hovered before his lips covered hers.

She remembered a great deal from the night they spent together, but this kiss was something she'd never experienced before. Warm and soft, Cal's lips claimed hers, surely at first, as if he wanted there to be no mistake that this kiss was no teenage pity party, that it had zilch to do with anything but the two of them, right here, right now.

Once Cal was sure he'd made himself perfectly clear on that score, the kiss gentled to nibbles that allowed him to ask questions and Gabby to answer without saying a word.

More?

Definitely.

Can you feel how much I want you?

Yes....

Beneath the sky and stars that looked as if they were taking their places to enjoy the show below, Cal and Gabby kissed not like desperate teens, but like a man and woman who knew exactly what they were doing and why.

No one else has ever made me feel like this. That was the single thought that broke through the haze of Gabby's desire.

She had waited fifteen years to kiss a man passionately for the second time, and she realized quickly that the wait had been absolutely worth it.

Chapter Ten

With adrenaline making her fingers shaky, Gabby had to concentrate to open her front door and flick on the light. Cal followed her into her cozy bungalow and shut the door behind them.

With a hundred-watt bulb instead of starlight illuminating Cal's face, Gabby saw the physical hunger in his eyes quite clearly, and her own body responded as it had been for the past three blocks.

"Are you sure your babysitter can stay later?" Gabby asked, hearing the breathlessness in her voice.

"'Preteen caretaker,'" he corrected, walking forward and running a finger along the bodice of her scoop-neck blouse. Light as a feather, his touch sent goose bumps skittering along her skin. "She said she could stay until ten."

"The dance class only lasts until eight."

"I thought we might get coffee afterward."

"Do you want coffee?"

"No."

Gabby's sleeveless blouse had skinny white and turquoise ribbons that crisscrossed up the front, making it more formfitting. With a thumb and forefinger, Cal pulled ever so slowly on the bow tied at the neckline, and it unraveled as if it were melting. The loosened bodice provided easier access to her lacy bra and the bosom it cupped, and within seconds Cal's hand replaced the material.

The warmth of his palm, the teasing of his thumb made Gabby moan, and that moan was all it took to lure his mouth once more to hers as he bent to lift her into his arms.

Gabby was not a small woman, but she felt like a sylph with Cal's muscles supporting her and with his earlier gentleness replaced by a voracious appetite. No question where they were headed now.

"Which way?" he said.

Reluctantly, she patted his shoulder. *Oh, those muscles!* "Better put me down. The bedrooms are upstairs," she told him between little gasps as he nuzzled her neck.

Cal lifted his head. When he located the stairs, he headed toward them, still carrying her, silencing her protest with more kisses. How he managed not to break his neck was beyond her, but he seemed to have no problem walking upstairs without looking where he was going, and his kisses were so delicious that Gabby didn't care whether she was in imminent danger of tumbling down the stairs. Even if Cal proved to be as sure-footed as a goat, she knew she was in danger of falling hard for her one and only lover.

In the bedroom, Cal set her on the bed and followed her down. As he kissed her from her neck to her breasts, she drowned in the sensations. Had it felt this way last time? Her hands slid up his back and then into his hair. After cutting men's hair professionally for thirteen years, one

head was pretty much like another, but delving her fingers
into Cal's thick, wavy locks and cupping the back of his
head while he pressed onto her skin kisses that seemed
to shoot straight through to her soul—that was a brand-
spankin'-new experience.

"This needs to come off," Cal muttered, reaching for
the hem of her top and pulling it over her head.

She helped him then ordered, "Now yours."

Panting when the job was done, they looked at each
other. *Heavens,* Gabby thought. Just…*heavens.*

Because only a divine source could have made a man
as beautiful as Cal. It was that same masculine splendor
that had made her want to put a barrier between them
when she was an awkward young teen. Cal's handsome-
ness wasn't perfect like Dean's; it was rough around the
edges, earthy and muscled and teeming with power. Dean
had been her fantasy, a prince charming who would dance
with her to the sound of bluebirds tweeting. She'd imagined their relationship being so easy.

Cal was real.

*What a difference a decade—and some heartache—
can make.* Today, she craved *real.*

Reaching up, Gabby traced Cal's pecs with no small
sense of awe. Cal tensed, his jaw clenched and shivered.
Actually shivered.

Gabby grinned; she couldn't help it. She felt wonderfully powerful with her fingertips reading his muscles as
if they were Braille.

"Do you like that?" she asked in what she hoped was
a husky, goddess-of-sex voice.

She'd flipped on the light so he could see where he was
going as they entered the room and now she could see the
glint of humor and hunger in his eyes. He nodded down
at her without speaking. She liked to think he couldn't.

Wow, you'd think I'd been doing this awhile. I—

"Oh, no!" Gabby sat up so quickly, she nearly flipped Cal off her.

He rolled to the side, placing a hand on her stomach in concern. "What? What's wrong?"

His touch made her belly quiver. "We need... I don't have any..."

Bracing himself, Cal sat up all the way. "I have a condom." He reached for her again, but she said, "I've heard those aren't very effective for birth control...if that's all you use."

Cal hesitated. "You don't have any other birth control?"

She shook her head.

"Nothing?"

"No."

Sitting on the foot of the bed, Cal leaned over his knees, taking deep breaths. After a moment, he reached out to massage her leg, one of his brows arched in curiosity. "No boyfriends in a while?"

A simple "No" would have sufficed, but Gabby knew this was the fork in the road: She could protect her ego or tell him the whole truth.

There wasn't much time to ponder, so she listened to her gut, and her gut said that Cal, of all people, deserved honesty.

"No boyfriends in a...uh..."

Damn, this was not going to be easy. What if he thought she was pathetic? What if he preferred not to have sex with women whose inexperience put the burden of creating a pleasurable experience on him? What if—

"No boyfriends *ever*," she blurted, forcing herself to maintain eye contact.

Cal squeezed one eye half shut. He tilted his head. "*Ever*? As in...not since us?"

"Technically, we never dated," she pointed out. "But that's the gist of it."

They sat in silence—his, pensive; hers, as uncomfortable as a sofa cushion made of needles. She could see him trying to work out how it was possible, in this day and age, for a woman not planning to enter a religious order to have remained celibate as long as she had. And then his expression ripened with awareness and disbelief.

"You stayed loyal to him all these years?"

Gabby shook her head. "That may have been part of it at first, but…no. I didn't stay single only because I was waiting for Dean." Despite some difficulty in making her voice work, she told him what she'd figured out lately, stumbling over the words she was determined to get out. "I stayed single because I was too disappointed in myself to believe a really good man would be interested in me." She looked at her hands—big-boned with long, capable fingers and neat nails that were practically short, square and unpolished. "For as long as I can remember, I've felt kind of inept when it comes to being a woman. I mean, I grew up hoping to be Cinderella or Sleeping Beauty and instead I turned out more like Pippi Longstocking meets Laura Ingalls. Growing up pudgy and shy didn't help."

Cal had been listening attentively, but now arched a brow. "You? Shy?" He shook his head. "As I recall, you were pretty damn bossy, Gabby."

She stared then laughed. "Thanks a lot."

He patted her thigh—nothing sexual, just a reassuring stroke. "I'm just saying, you never saw yourself accurately. Not the way others saw you."

She should be happy, she supposed, that he wasn't reacting too strongly to the revelation that he was her one and only lover. She shrugged. "Well. Whether I was right or wrong about the way other people saw me, I wasted a lot of time trying to live a fairy tale instead of joining the real world."

He nodded. "And now you want to do something about it."

"Yes, I do. That doesn't reflect well on me. Or on what we were going to do tonight, does it?" She shook her head. "Fifteen years ago, I used you to get over Dean. Now it seems I'm using you again."

Cal narrowed his gaze. "To start your life? That's not exactly unflattering," he answered, surprising her.

"I bring a lot of baggage to a relationship. All that in-experience."

With a crooked smile, he tucked a long red curl behind her ear. "That's not baggage, honey. That's a challenge."

Reaching up to take his hand, she brought it to her lap and held it with both of hers. "Fifteen years ago, I had no idea how I felt about you. Now I know that I was attracted to you, and that it scared me." She looked at his large hand, tucked between hers. "It still scares me."

"Why?"

"You can predict the outcome of a romantic fairy tale. I don't have any idea what will happen with us."

All Gabby heard for several seconds was the sound of Cal's breathing, heavier than it had been moments before. With his free hand, he covered hers and squeezed. "You of all people ought to know the answer to that," he said, his voice a sandpapery whisper that scratched through the silence. "Your grandfather used to say it all the time, 'The past is history, the future's a mystery, the present is a gift.'" Raising their clasped hands, he kissed her tense knuckles. "Unwrapping gifts too soon—that's always been my downfall."

Which meant, Gabby figured, that the extraordinary-physical-sensations part of the evening was over, at least for now. But then Cal smiled, roguish light dancing in his eyes.

"On the other hand," he said, "this is one gift I've waited fifteen years to enjoy."

Unclasping their hands, he drew hers gently around his waist until they rested on his lower back, which brought her conveniently into his arms. Reverently, his fingers combed her sculpted red curls off her forehead, giving him a clear canvas on which to press kiss upon kiss... upon kiss.

Gabby melted beneath his lips. Eventually, they fell back on the bed, and she realized that he was still naked from the waist up and that she was about to be.

Releasing her face, his deft fingers reached beneath her to unhook her bra and push it down, revealing the nipple his mouth was seeking.

As if he was unwrapping a gift bit by bit, savoring the anticipation, investigating each small portion as if it were a puzzle piece he needed to study—that's exactly how he made her feel. Untutored as they were, Gabby's hands moved across his back, up his ribcage, across the skin that was smooth and firm and gloriously tan, until he stopped her by reaching for her hands and placing them by her side.

"Just enjoy this," he whispered.

"I am," she assured, barely able to catch her breath, her restless hands moving to him. She felt him tense as her fingers pressed into his back.

"Trust me," he gritted, his voice as tense as his muscles now, "you don't want to do that unless you want this to end much too soon."

Gabby had closed her eyes but it sounded as if he was smiling.

Pressing her hands firmly back to the bed, he returned

to the exploration *he* felt perfectly free to pursue. Fingers slipping smoothly beneath her skirt, he reached for her, eliciting a gasp from Gabby and making it virtually impossible for her to keep her hands still. She clenched the bedspread.

He remembered about the birth control, didn't he?

Apparently…yes.

Gabby's eyes opened wide as Cal proceeded to make love to her without any need for birth control whatsoever.

For someone as inexperienced as she, it was…a revelation. A catapulting into a world of sensation she'd never imagined before. It was—

Amazing.

As the passion mounted higher, Gabby felt herself being led into a vortex of emotions—excitement and joy, confusion and uncertainty and, for a moment, near panic. She and Cal could never, ever be mere friends again. They were complicating their lives impossibly, with no road back. Once a heart awakened, it could so easily be broken. And still she followed him along the path.

Willingly.

The clock above Gabby's workstation had a comb and pair of barbering shears instead of hands. Currently the comb was on the twelve and the scissors pointed squarely toward the eleven. Five minutes to noon.

Which meant it had been thirteen hours and fifty-five minutes since she'd last seen the man who had become her second lover…or did he still qualify as her first lover? Either way, Cal had helped her feel sexier last night than she ever had in her life or ever thought she could feel. And in retrospect Gabby realized that the feeling of worth, of being cherished, had had little to do with sexual prowess, hers or his (although his was really stellar, even without having anything else to compare it to). No, she had spent the entire morning feeling more womanly than ever before, because Cal's touch had been both carnal and reverently tender. And because, even though he hadn't asked for anything in return, he had responded to her unskilled offerings like a man who'd been in prison for years and just received a full pardon.

She couldn't stop thinking about him. Couldn't concentrate on much of anything. She had no idea whether she was supposed to call him or wait for him to phone her. Were they going to see each other again the way they had seen each other last night—exposed physically and emotionally? Navigating a relationship was like finding one's way through a corn maze blindfolded and dizzy.

Redoubling her efforts to focus on her current client, Gabby finished the David Beckham buzz he'd asked for by carefully tidying his neck area with her electric clippers.

"You're taking me to lunch," she told her brother as she finished his cut. "Lesley's got me on a diet, and I'm starving."

Eyes closed, arms folded beneath the black cape protecting his clothes, Ben offered no resistance, but asked, "Do I have to tip you, too?"

"Yes, and it serves you right for dating your regular barber. When are you going to learn?"

"Learn what? That I shouldn't date women with scissors or that from now on I ought to get my hair cut by men?"

Pausing long enough to cuff her brother upside the head, she answered, "That you shouldn't dump women after you sleep with them. It's rude."

Lord, what if Cal dumped her now that they'd been intimate? Not that they'd actually "slept" together yet; he'd left by ten as he'd had a babysitter to send home. And without adequate birth control, they hadn't actually done IT. They'd done everything but IT, though.

They'd made no promises to each other, of course, and wouldn't. She would be leaving in two months; he had his daughter and a new job on which to concentrate. But if he ended things with her now...oh, that would feel awful.

She punched Ben in the shoulder. "That's from every girlfriend you've ever been physically intimate with and then dumped."

Reluctantly, Ben's eyes opened. As usual, he couldn't be bothered to react too strongly. "I don't 'dump' women. I tell them—in person, by the way, no texting involved—that I'm not getting married, ever. Occasionally, they take it personally."

"Fancy that."

"Yeah." Ben shrugged beneath the cape, closing his eyes again, giving the appearance of a man who was utterly relaxed.

It was so easy for Ben to score date after date after eager date. Women flirted outrageously with him. Gabby had seen it. In restaurants, in a shopping mall, even in church, Ben had his pick of available females. His relationships ambled along, and the women didn't get upset by his laissez-faire ways until they realized he really, truly wasn't in it for the long haul. Then the dating doo-doo hit the fan.

"Women are not picky enough," Gabby muttered.

Ben opened one eye. "You're besmirching me again, aren't you?"

"Just trying to figure out why we girls are so desperate to be in love that we'll moon after men who are completely unavailable."

Ben rested with his eyes shut while Gabby removed his

cape and paper collar and used a brush to remove stray hairs from his suit shirt. "Because we unavailable boys keep your fantasies of romance alive. We don't take out garbage, we don't fix the leaks under your sink with our plumbers' cracks showing—"

"Ben!"

"—and we don't badger the women we're with about how many lights are left on or whether the windows are shut when the air-conditioning's running. Because we don't care. We're the perfect companions. We're actually performing a service—keeping romance alive. Then you all want to get *serious,* and blame us when the romance dies. If you think about it, we men are the victims here."

Gabby stared. "What did our happily married parents ever do to wind up with four out of five commitment-phobic offspring?"

"Beats me. Are you a commitment phobe?"

"I'm thirty-three and unmarried. The evidence is there."

"You know how to take care of yourself. I've always admired that."

"Thanks."

She watched Ben brush a few stray hairs off his sleeve. He seemed utterly uninterested in whether his new 'do flattered him—which, of course, it did. The inherited bone structure Gabby considered overly strong on her, made Ben's face a work of art. Resembling Paul Newman in his prime, Ben could wear hair past his shoulders or go completely bald and not affect his sex appeal one iota. For him, beauty was simply a given—and, thankfully, something with which he appeared not to concern himself. Not that Ben got riled about anything. Was there a woman—somewhere—destined to break through the ennui that seemed to shroud her big bro'?

"Speaking of women and romance," Gabby said, "Lesley wants me to ask if you'll take her ballroom class—free of charge. There's a single woman who needs a partner. And this is not a setup. Honest."

Rising from the chair, Ben reached for the tie he'd removed prior to the haircut. "Gabrielle, dearest, I'd like to attend ballroom classes almost as much as I want to tie my carotid artery into a slipknot. Almost."

"Oh, Ben, dance lessons are good for you. They're character-building. And women love a man who can dance."

Ben arched one deeply profound eyebrow.

Right. Why make the effort when women already flocked to him?

"I fear for your immortal soul," Gabby said, wondering if she should insist that he help Lesley and the very shy dance student, but before she could nudge him again, the door to the barbershop opened.

"Hey, Cal, buddy!" Ben smiled into the mirror before him, able to see the new arrival. "You're just in time."

Gabby turned her head, locking eyes with the man who entered the shop. A shot of adrenaline shook her heart.

He smiled at her, and the very air around him seemed to turn golden. It took a long time for him to glance Ben's way. "In time for what?"

"I'm taking Gabby to lunch. Want to come?"

Dang. How would they possibly sit through lunch without referring to last night? Already her hands itched to touch Cal. Before Gabby could figure out how to resolve her suddenly full social calendar, Cal raised the two white paper bags he was carrying. "I brought lunch. I was hoping to talk Gabby into taking a break."

"You were?" Ben said.

He was?

"Yep. I stopped by The Stinger and picked up Irish nachos." He looked right at her.

He remembers. A hometown fast-food shack, The Stinger made Irish nachos that had been Gabby's favorite food throughout her teens. Skinny fries blanketed in rich melted cheddar, bacon bits and scallions, they were served with a side of ranch dressing—a diet killer if ever there was one. Lesley had made Gabby swear off them. Then the fall of Gabby's junior year in high school, she'd contracted the chicken pox she had somehow managed to avoid previously. Her parents had brought her games to take her mind off the infernal itching; Lesley had brought her magazines; her brothers had asked if they could play connect-the-dots with a Sharpie and Cal had shown up with an order of Irish nachos. Eating them had provided her only pleasurable moments.

"Did you bring a Stinger salad, too?" she asked now, her voice low and breathy.

Lips curling, he nodded and answered in an equally low voice. "With salted honey-roasted sunflower seeds."

If she hadn't experienced it herself, Gabby would never have believed that talking about food could feel like foreplay. Cal's eyes sparkled with an intimacy and promise more delicious than any meal.

Fortunately, Ben was focusing most of his attention on knotting his tie, but he did mutter, "I haven't had Irish nachos in years." Finished with making himself more beautiful, he turned. "Open the bags, buddy. The fries can be an appetizer."

"How do you know you're invited?" Gabby teased her confident elder brother. She had no intention of truly kicking Ben to the curb, but being alone with Cal sounded mighty fine.

"I'm always invited, Gabrielle. When are you going

to accept that I'm irresistible company?" Ben grinned, though their conversation appeared to have knocked a bit of the happy-go-lucky out of him.

"Actually, Ben, I need to talk to Gabby alone." Cal looked at her. "Unless you want me to come back another time?"

Halfway to the nachos bag, Ben stopped and split his gaze between Cal and his sister.

Happy and tense at once, Gabby smiled in response to his curious gaze, wondering how much to divulge to her brother. Cal took care of the dilemma for her.

"Gabby's helping me with my daughter. I wanted to fine-tune a few things we discussed last night." He remained straight-faced as he looked at her.

They hadn't discussed Minna much at all the previous evening except with regard to the babysitter. She wondered what he wanted to "fine-tune"? Last night they'd played pretty good music together, but if he wanted to improve on what was already accomplished, okay by her!

"You mind if I pass on lunch, Ben?"

Ben staggered, a hand on his chest as if he were feeling for a heartbeat. "Whoa. My company rejected? Irish nachos denied?" He pointed a finger at each of them. "This is a first."

Unbowed, Cal offered his friend one of the white bags. "Gabby and I can share an order."

"No, thank you." Ben held up a hand. He crossed to pluck his jacket from the coat tree. "I'll go see the parents. I spoke to Dad earlier. He's grumpy, because Mom will only feed him fish and salad. I'll stop by Honey Bea's, pick up a couple of Kaiser rolls and join him." He tapped Cal's arm on his way to the door. "I'm taking the parents back to Bend with me so they'll be closer to the hospital for check-in tomorrow. You think you'll be able to stop by?"

"Absolutely. I'm planning on it."

"Good." Ben nodded, his gaze sliding to his sister. "Maybe you could drive Gabs. She might get a little emotional tomorrow."

"Hey, I'm right here," Gabby protested her brother's use of third person. "I can drive and be emotional. It's called multitasking."

The men did not protest. Ben kissed her on her cheek, said goodbye to Cal and headed to the door. Before he left, he glanced appraisingly at his sister and friend then reached for a sign that read "Breaks Are Good For You. Be Back Later," and hung it on the door handle. Grinning, he offered them a two-finger salute and headed out to sunny Main Street.

Cal set the bags of food on her desk then walked slowly toward Gabby. She couldn't focus on much other than his mouth, that full-lipped, deliciously hot mouth that had managed, without ever saying a word, to make her feel like the most beautiful woman on the planet.

"Do you think he suspects anything?" she asked, barely able to make her lips move and afraid they, too, might be quivering.

"If he does," Cal answered, speaking softly, "I trust him to be mature and discreet."

"Oh. You don't remember Ben well, do you?"

"I recall a few things over which he swore me to secrecy. I think he knows that when it comes to discretion, one hand washes the other." Humor curled Cal's lips and crinkled his eyes.

Oh, she wished Cal would reach for her. Casually dressed once again, he looked like a model hired to entice tourists to explore Oregon's great outdoors. As lean as he was tall, he possessed nonetheless the solid biceps and flat abdomen of an athlete. Small wonder that Gabby felt…things when he was nearby. Plenty of women would. Even the ones who hadn't already had sex with him.

It seemed her fingertips were going to be in a perennially itchy-to-touch-him state. She endeavored to keep them calm, so she wouldn't seem sex-starved. "So, Ben won't say anything, then. That's a relief," she murmured.

"He could shout our relationship to the rooftops as far as I'm concerned, if it wasn't for Minna. I know you want to keep things under wraps, though."

Actually, Gabby had experienced some shouting urges herself last night and this morning. She'd had to sit on her hands not to phone Lesley about the extraordinary turn of events and about…well, about how amazing-incredible-toe curling-fabulous-exhilarating sex had been. And, because of the missing birth control, they still had one bigger step to take. What were the chances it would actually get *better?*

Just as she decided to reach for him and practice the kissing skills she'd taken for a spin last night, Cal said, "Where do you want to eat?"

"Eat? Right now?"

"You hate cold Irish nachos," he murmured.

"Oh. True. They get soggy."

"Yep."

He'd taken a step closer. They could see each other's irises now.

"So we should eat." Frankly, she didn't care if she never ate another Irish nacho in her life. She lifted her arms to circle his neck.

"Gabby?"

"Mmm?"

"You have a plate-glass window in front of your store and customers who I bet never read that 'closed' sign. There's not much we can do in here unless we don't mind begin discovered."

"Oh." Halting the motion, she raised her brows. "Wow, you're practical."

"I have a child and you have parents and siblings to consider. It might be different if you were staying in town, but under the circumstances...." He shrugged apologetically, the voice of reason.

Angling his body, Cal trailed his upstage hand—the one farther from the window and presumably out of sight—slowly up Gabby's arm. Unmindful of the summer heat, her body reacted with goose bumps that skittered across her skin.

"Want to come over tonight?" he murmured in that tantalizing me-man, you-my-favorite-dessert voice of his. "The *I Love Lucy* marathon begins at seven."

"I—*I Love Lucy?* You want to watch *I Love Lucy?* Really?"

"I never kid about Lucy." He looped a red curl around his finger, still with the upstage hand. "Minna wants to see the Connecticut episodes. Come on, Gabby," he encouraged, so close to her ear now that she could feel his warm breath stir her hair. "We'll watch the Ricardos sleep in twin beds and feel their frustration. It's called a casual night at home."

She'd feel the frustration, all right.

After last night, she wanted more lovemaking. She could barely keep her hands off his body, yet he seemed to be perfectly in control.

"A casual night at home." Gabby swallowed hard. She did want to see Minna again and, moreover, had promised to get to know the girl better as part of their trade. Fair was fair. "An *I Love Lucy* marathon sounds fun. Sure."

"Great. In the meantime, where do you want me?"

Blinded by hunger for everything she'd felt the night before, all sorts of visual images hijacked her brain. "Where do I…uh…"

"Where should we sit down for lunch?"

"Oh. Right." She gestured limply toward the chairs lined up along the window. "We can sit there."

"Terrific." Cal stepped away from her with little apparent difficulty, whereas she felt as if they'd been buddy breathing from the same oxygen tank and he'd just walked off with it.

Act casually, she coached herself.

Cal had been married and divorced; he had a child. No telling how much sex he'd had in the previous decade and a half (probably a lot), so he obviously didn't feel the giddy excitement or the urgency she did every time she got close enough to smell a pheromone.

S'okay. Don't take it personally.

Mechanically, she helped him set out the food, a black cape tucked beneath the Styrofoam boxes to catch greasy drips.

"A barbershop picnic," he said when they were about to sit down. "This is a first. Thanks for spending your lunch hour with me, Gabby."

Her stomach did a backflip with a twist. How did he do that—smile with his eyes so that she felt like a ball of ice cream and his gaze seemed like a ribbon of hot fudge?

"Ready to dig in?"

"Sure," she lied. She could sit opposite him and she could act as if she was excited about her old favorite treat, but she doubted she'd be able to choke down a single cheese-drenched fry.

Lusting after Cal Wells had to be the best diet ever.

Chapter Eleven

Cal's second shower of the day occurred shortly after he left the barbershop. This one was ice-freaking cold. On purpose.

Being within shouting distance of Gabrielle Coombs without putting his hands all over her luscious body was difficult enough. Pretending he was perfectly content to share lunch instead of a bed—that required a performance worthy of a major award.

The plumbing fixtures squeaked as Cal turned off the water. Whipping a bath towel off the hook, he towel-dried while reminding himself why he hadn't whisked Gabby back to his place for a little afternoon delight, which had offered infinitely more appeal than fries with cheese and ranch dressing.

"Because you're keeping your eye on the big picture."

Unable to work with his mind racing a million miles an hour and his pants far too snug for comfort, he'd headed home for a shower and to set the stage for part two of The Seduction of Gabby Coombs. He did have a plan, after all.

Dressing in jeans and a T-shirt, he abandoned the idea of going back to work and headed downstairs to prep for this evening.

Anyone could find a lover for an hour…a night…a few weeks…a year. Cal wanted something else. Always had.

Gabby Coombs represented what he'd lacked all his life—stability. Not the stability that came from a robust bank account and clever investments, but rather the kind that budded from a connection transcending time and place.

Walking through the first floor of his humble rented house, he compared it to the hovel in which he'd grown up and the showplace in Chicago that his ex-wife had decorated. Cal knew without a doubt that he hadn't found "home" yet. That feeling was something he still wanted for himself, something he swore he would provide for Minna.

Entering the kitchen, prepared to set the stage for the kind of evening he hoped to repeat many times in his life, Cal pictured a woman with corkscrew red hair, about a trillion quotes on the tip of her tongue and a smile that put the sun to shame.

Home. He felt it best when he thought of his Gabby.

"I forgot that Betty Grable guest-starred on *I Love Lucy.*" Cozy as all get out on the sofa in Cal's living room, Gabby sat between her host and his daughter, a bowl of fresh raspberry gelato—homemade by the gentleman of the house—on her lap, her heart humming with a content-ment that rather fascinated her.

"Who's Betty Grable? Was she famous?" Minna asked,

taking a big spoonful of her own gelato, which she'd sprinkled liberally with mini chocolate chips.

"Betty Grable was a singer, dancer and actress," Cal answered. "At the peak of her popularity, young men all over the world bought her poster, which made her known as a 'pin-up' girl."

Gabby had spent a number of relaxed evenings in this house when it had belonged to Claire Dobbs before she'd become Claire Kingsley. Always, the theme of those visits had been family, with Claire's three kiddos featuring prominently in the evening. Gabby had enjoyed the atmosphere in the modest home immensely, but never as much as she was enjoying tonight.

Minna had a relationship with her father that encompassed all the best qualities of the parent-child bond. While Cal was clearly the final word in the household, he was also playful, gregarious, an out-and-out jokester at times, plus as warm and relaxing as a summer day. In the presence of this father-daughter duo, Gabby felt as if she were being lulled into a state of ease and pleasure. All through the evening, she felt herself lowering a guard she heretofore hadn't realized she'd raised.

"Betty Grable was especially famous for her legs," she offered as she licked the back of her gelato spoon. "She was nicknamed The Girl With The Million Dollar Legs, and—"

Oh, Lord. Gabby's throat seemed to close as she realized her gaffe.

Glancing at Cal first, she shot him a look of profound apology. She felt like an insensitive oaf! Cal had already told her that, at age ten, Minna was beginning to feel insecure about the differences her CP imposed upon her, and those differences centered, of course, on her legs— their behavior if not their appearance.

Sensing her distress, and perhaps the imminent threat that she might dig a deeper hole if she started to hyper-babble, Cal discreetly reached out to squeeze her arm.

"Betty's gams were legendary, all right," he concurred, speaking with utter casualness, "but they had nothing on you ladies."

Minna frowned at the television. "What are gams?"

"Another word for legs." Cal maintained a cheerful, matter-of-fact tone.

Minna nodded. "I like it. It sounds kind of mechanical. Like my legs—sometimes they move like they have motors."

Laughing freely, Cal winked at Gabby. *See? No harm done.*

Admiration for the amazing team of father and daughter filled her, admiration and a deep longing to participate in the life they were creating. She wondered whether she should mention the Miss You Can Do It Pageant or wait until she'd okayed the topic with Cal first. She'd looked it up on the internet early that morning and discovered not only that the next pageant was coming up, but that Minna still had time to enter.

"Fourth of July is around the corner," Cal said before she could decide whether to mention Miss You Can Do It. "Minna and I were wondering whether you'd like to join us for a picnic, Gabby."

Fourth of July. Forever the anniversary of her first sexual experience—with the man beside her.

She looked at him and the moment she did, she knew he was thinking the very same thing. He had the most amazing way of staring at her with his eyes aflame even though the rest of him appeared utterly calm.

Were they going to make love again before the big anniversary night? Cal had been as sweet to her tonight as he'd been to his daughter. But sweet wasn't all she wanted from him. When she was with Cal, she wanted… She wanted…

"Please say yes, Gabby," Minna implored. "Dad makes, like, forty pounds of potato salad every year. If we don't finish it on the Fourth of July, then I have to have it for lunch every day until Halloween."

Gabby turned to Cal. "Are you really that cruel?"

He jerked back, wounded. "Cruel? First, I'll have you know that my potato salad is as legendary as Betty Grable's gams. Second, the child grossly exaggerates the facts. I made a measly ten pounds last summer, and she didn't have to eat a bite beyond September first."

Nodding to Minna, Gabby promised, "I won't abandon you. We'll pawn the potato salad off on my brothers."

"Pinky swear?"

Gabby linked her little finger with Minna's.

Cal pretended to be offended, but she caught him trading winks with Minna.

Warm, sweet honey flowed through Gabby's veins. Father and daughter were working as a team to keep her in their lives. And she didn't mind. She didn't mind one little bit.

At ten o'clock, Minna started to yawn copiously. She didn't protest when Cal announced it was time to head upstairs. Father stayed put on the couch while daughter moved drowsily to pick up her crutches. Cal did not immediately attempt to help, which surprised Gabby. Moving with her crutches, the little girl headed sleepily for the stairs while Cal watched from his place on the sofa.

"I could help you just for tonight," he offered. To Gabby, he explained, "Usually Minna gets herself upstairs."

Surprised and impressed, Gabby nodded. She was equally impressed when Minna looked at her father, dimples appearing in her cheeks. "Okay. You can help me. But only for tonight. You're not allowed to ask tomorrow."

"Deal. But don't make me pinky swear. That's girly."

Rolling her eyes at Gabby, Minna complained, "Fathers."

When Cal rose and bent over the couch to scoop her up, Minna went happily into her dad's strong arms.

"Say good-night, Min," he instructed before he headed for the stairs.

"Good night, Min," his daughter responded on cue. After Gabby laughed, Minna rested her cheek sleepily on Cal's shoulder and said, "'Night, Gabby. I'm glad you came over."

"Me, too, sweetie. I had a wonderful time. 'Night, Cal," she said reluctantly. Intending to leave the duo to their nighttime routine, she rose. "I'll see myself out."

"Don't go," Cal countered quickly. "If I know my daughter, she'll be asleep before her beautiful head hits the pillow."

Min nodded. "Yep. And then Dad'll be lonely." She yawned hugely. "He needs adult conversation so his brain won't rot."

Cal shrugged his eyebrows wryly at Gabby. "You heard her. You're all that stands between me and brain rot. It's your humanitarian duty to stay."

Gabby assented with a nod, and Minna snuggled into her father as he carried her up the stairs. For the next fifteen minutes, Gabby cleaned up, clearing their gelato bowls and tidying the kitchen. Lost in her thoughts, she didn't realize Cal had returned until he slipped behind her to turn the water off in the sink and circle his arms around her waist.

"You don't have to clean my dishes."

The whispered words tickled her neck, sending shivers

racing down her spine. "I helped get them dirty," she said, though she couldn't summon the will to turn the water on again.

Turning her in his arms, Cal touched her forehead and nose with his. "I can think of a much better use of your time."

"For example?"

"For example, a whole lot of necking."

"Sounds wonderful…."

And frustrating, she thought an hour later after Cal had kissed her so wonderfully and so thoroughly that she was sure she could feel every pore in her body singing. She wanted to get in touch with every one of his pores, too— right away and without his clothes getting in the way. Cal seemed much, much more in control than she felt.

"What time should I pick you up tomorrow?" he murmured as they stood by her car, saying good-night.

"Tomorrow?" Did they really have to wait that long to see each other again?

"I'm driving you to the hospital in Bend, remember?"

She hadn't forgotten her father's surgery, but she couldn't recall having made the decision to ride with Cal. "I'll probably be there all day and evening. You've got Minna to think about. It's too much—"

"Irene's meeting her at the bus stop. Min will be at camp most of the day then she and Irene are going to make an obscene amount of cookie dough for the July Fourth bake sale. It's all taken care of. All you have to do is tell me what time to pick you up. I'll even bring you a latte." He bent toward her as they leaned against her car, but didn't touch, seducing her with his voice alone and the mundane offer of coffee. "Skim, double-shot, with sugar-free vanilla."

"That's just how I like it."

"I know."

"How?"

"I know everything about you, Gabby Coombs."

The night was fragrant with the jasmine Claire had planted along the side of the house when she'd lived here. Stars filled the ebony sky, glittering so brightly they might have been twinkle lights strung directly above their heads.

Something magical seemed to stir inside Gabby, some sense of wonder and hope she wasn't sure she'd ever felt before tonight, before this very instant.

Cal kissed her good-night gently, a sweet ending to the evening rather than a prelude to something more, but she didn't mind; the moment seemed to call for sweetness. She drove home, to the house she'd lived in solo for ten years. For the first time in…oh, lordy, maybe for the first time ever, she didn't feel alone.

She felt whole. There wasn't a thing about herself she would change tonight. Two very real, singularly strong and decent people had drawn her into their world, and she hadn't wanted to leave. She'd belonged there, had clicked into the puzzle of their lives without force, manipulation or fantasy.

I know everything about you, Cal had said.

Caleb Wells—so real, so imperfectly just what the doctor ordered—had always seen her exactly as she was.

Gabby wasn't sure what it all meant, but, perhaps for the first time in her life, she didn't think she needed to know. Beyond any plans she made with her mind, she longed to follow her heart, and right now it was leading her straight into Cal's arms.

"My father is incorrigible. Who asks for pastrami when they're still emerging from anesthesia?"

Spending the bulk of the day in a hospital waiting room

with her nervous family had taken its toll on Gabby. Noticeably weary, she sagged in the passenger seat of Cal's sedan as they headed back to Honeyford.

Cal was grateful for her father's ill-advised, but gratifyingly lively request. Frank had put everyone more at ease by awakening from surgery with his vulnerable arteries cleaned and his crusty exterior still intact.

He and Lesley had ferried coffee and sandwiches to the Coombs crew. He'd held hands and patted shoulders, and it had made him feel needed by the family *he* had needed so desperately during his teens. The payback was gratifying. Even better, everything he did for Gabby felt like food for his soul; helping her in the simplest ways filled him, satisfied him, made him hungry to do more.

She wanted to make love with him; that had been clear for the past few days. Resisting continued to be an act of Herculean effort. Had to do it, though, because sex, especially great sex, could be damned distracting. First, he needed her to see how well they fit into each other's dull days, all the busy boring moments. He wanted her to see that mundane turned to magic when it was infused with love.

He wanted her to choose to stay.

"Do you want dinner?" he asked, glancing over and finding Gabby's eyes closed.

"I'm not particularly hungry," she answered without opening her eyes. "But if you want to stop somewhere, I can get something to drink."

"I'm not hungry, either," he said. "How about driving through Starbucks before we head back?"

"Sure."

They ordered blended drinks, introducing a welcome chill to the hot evening. Gabby's drink melted when she nodded off on the hour-long return trip to Honeyford, however. Cal let her sleep, knowing she'd expended a great deal of energy worrying during her father's surgery.

Pulling into her driveway, he cut the engine and moved around the car to the passenger-side door. Opening it, he crouched down, intending to gently wake her, but reconsidered as her soft lips puffed out adorably with her breath. A tiny furrow pinched her brow as she slept.

Years from now, that little line would be a wrinkle and, though he'd never use the word "wrinkle" in front of her, he realized how damn much he wanted to grow old looking at Gabby. Watching her smile and watching her sleep. Seeing laugh lines and frown lines and knowing he was encoded in every one.

"You have no idea how I feel, do you?" he whispered, reaching into the car to smooth those crazy red curls off her forehead.

It was still light out and would be for a couple more hours. It was not inconceivable that someone could walk by and see him touching Gabby more like a lover than a friend, and he knew she didn't want that, not yet, anyway. Nor would it be good for Minna, who was coming to relish Gabby's company, to believe there was potential for permanence in their relationship if she was destined to be disappointed in the end. But for this instant, Cal couldn't help himself. Touching Gabby seemed as essential as inhaling.

For only two people had Cal felt the kind of tenderness that made his heart ache like any muscle given a good workout. He felt it with Minna, of course; but he'd felt it first with Gabby, so many years ago. And again now.

Nothing he'd ever tried—not the exercising of strict mental discipline or leaving town or even marrying someone else—had deflected his desire to be with this one woman.

Resigned, Cal ran the back of his hand gently along her cheek. "Time to wake up, Sleeping Beauty. You're home."

Gabby turned her head toward his hand, snuggling farther into the seat.

He smiled and tried again, receiving pretty much the same response.

"Okey dokey," he said, reaching for her purse and examining the zippered pockets until he found her house keys.

Rising, Cal strode up her walkway, opened her front door then returned to the car to sling her purse over his shoulder and lift Gabby into his arms. He carried her over the threshold, kicked the door shut and headed toward her bedroom.

Temptation was a powerful thing, but Cal managed to ignore the thoughts Gabby's bed brought to mind. Or, if not to ignore, at least to resist them...until, bending low over the bed as he set her down, he felt her arms tighten around his neck.

She murmured again, as softly as she had in the car, but this time her words were crystal clear. "Don't go."

He pulled back enough to see Gabby's gray eyes watching him with heart-stopping need.

"Kiss me, Cal."

Hunger shot through him like a cannon explosion. "Are you awake?"

She nodded. A small smile played around her lips. "I think parts of me are more conscious than others, but yeah, I'm awake."

Pressure on the back of his neck said she was going for that kiss, and, oh, how he wanted to accommodate. There were things, however, a man his age learned about himself, like not to start something he knew damn well he wouldn't be able to stop.

He was about to remind her of their birth control issues and to confess that he could not, at the moment, handle an episode like the one two days ago, but she beat him to the punch.

"There's a community health clinic in Prineville. I went yesterday before I opened the shop."

Cal raised a brow, to which she nodded.

Oh, man.

The resolution he'd considered so carefully shriveled like paper set afire.

Gabby's arms tugged again and this time Cal obeyed. When had a drowning man refused a lifesaver? He pressed his lips to hers, groaning when she opened her mouth, discovering anew that nothing was sweeter to him than the taste of her, the feel. With one knee resting outside her thigh and one between her legs, he let her feel his weight and his desire while he delved his hands into the thick curls he adored. He spoke to her with his lips and his tongue and his hands—reaching beneath the hem of her yellow sundress, exploring her like a treasure he'd just unearthed then releasing the tiny buttons on the bodice— until there was only one place left for them to go.

They finished undressing with choppy, hungry movements and took a moment simply to revel in the feeling of skin against skin. When that became too painful to endure, they locked gazes and clasped fingers and took the plunge into waters they'd left uncharted all their lives— until now.

Heart-thumping sex and soul-searing emotion came together in one monumental act of giving themselves to each other wholly, nothing held back. And when it was done, Cal knew why the French used the phrase "little death" to refer to the final moment of sex.

Making love to Gabby, Cal felt undeniably as if he had died, glimpsed heaven and had been allowed to come back to earth reborn.

Chapter Twelve

Dressed in a cherry-red shirt beneath a royal-blue-and-white-striped summer jacket, Ben Kramer commenced his annual delivery of the Declaration of Independence into a microphone that boomed the founding fathers' principles throughout Doc Kingsley Memorial Park.

The Honeyford Days parade, featuring Lesley's choreography of her intrepid senior tappers, had already marched through downtown. Fletcher Kingsley, garbed as Uncle Sam, had done duty as the parade's Grand Marshal. The cotton-candy machine provided by Sherm's Queen Bee market was getting a workout over by the picnic tables.

Gabby had attended thirty-two Fourth of July celebrations in Honeyford. Today, in the company of Cal and his daughter, she was having the time of her life.

"You cannot eat all that." She laughed at Minna who sat at one of the tables with a huge cone of cotton candy,

pink as a rosebud, a foot-long hot dog smothered in Fred
Werblow's gold-medal-winning chili and a basket of Irish
nachos, to which her father had recently introduced her.

"Yeah, I can," she insisted, washing a glob of cotton
candy down with iced lemonade. "I'm ten."

"That's right." Cal nodded, his own plate empty after
he inhaled two hot dogs and a heaping scoop of the potato
salad he and Gabby had spent a good portion of the previous day preparing. "She's ten, and she has my DNA, so
she's inherited the human vacuum gene. Which reminds
me—Irene and Minna's cookies are available at the bake
sale, and I'm ready for dessert."

Gabby, who was still working on her chili-cheese dog,
shook her head and grinned.

A day that could have been fraught with complications
for her and Cal was turning out to be a collection of simple
delights. The fifteenth anniversary of their first time together was, at long last, an occasion to enjoy. They hadn't
made love since their union a few days before, because
they hadn't had a chance to be alone. Somehow, though,
that hadn't diminished the excitement of being together.

Yesterday, Cal had shown her how to make his "famous" potato salad while Minna worked on the computer
in her room. They'd stolen kisses and brushed against each
other far more than conditions in the roomy kitchen required. Today, not holding Cal's hand was one of the most
difficult things she'd ever done. Protecting their privacy
was starting to seem far less important than touching him
again. Watching Ben Kramer at the microphone, Gabby
entertained a brief fantasy in which she pulled the mike
from Ben's hands and told all of Honeyford that she and
Cal were an item. But they did not live in a vacuum. There
was Minna to consider, plus her own family.

There was the fact that she was still planning to leave. And that she and Cal had not talked about the future.

"Hey, Minna Butterfly." Cal drew his daughter's attention then nodded toward a group of girls her age. "Aren't those some of the girls from your camp?"

When Minna followed her father's gaze, her smile faltered.

Knowing Minna had seemed happier at camp lately, Gabby looked curiously at the girls. There were four. Dressed in shorts and tank tops, laughing as they played in the park's modest water feature, they seemed like colts in a field—active and free.

With support, Minna could stand in the fountain. If the girls helped her, she'd be able to laugh and play with them. Was she afraid to admit her dependence and ask for help?

Studying the preteens as they splashed around, Gabby was struck by a significant difference between them and Minna. As young as they were, Minna's friends exuded confidence, an unselfconscious exuberance. They wore boldly colored tank tops and shorts that showed off their long, strong legs. Two of the girls wore anklets and one had what appeared to be her entire collection of Silly Bandz around her wrist.

By contrast, Minna wore an oversize white T-shirt with an Oregon Ducks logo and loose khaki Capri pants. She'd pulled her mink-brown hair into a low ponytail that did little to enhance her natural beauty or evince any interest in grooming beyond a need to get clean.

Well, of course, Gabby realized. *Her mother left when she was still too young to care much about her appearance. And Cal is terrific, but his talents don't run to the personal styling of little girls.*

"Want me to see if they can come over?" Cal asked, referring to Minna's camp mates.

Gabby cringed even before Minna insisted in a heated whisper, "No! Geez, Dad."

Discreetly, beneath the picnic table, Gabby patted her lover on the knee, easily forgiving him this dorky dad moment. Aloud, she said, "Hey, Minna, I've been meaning to ask whether you're busy next Sunday."

"I don't think so," the girl mumbled, taking her attention off her friends and picking at the Irish nachos. "Are we?" she asked her father.

"This isn't a group event," Gabby interjected before Cal could respond. "Sorry, big guy." She shrugged. "Girls only."

Minna perked up. "Really?"

"Yes. Are you free?"

At Cal's nod, Minna smiled. "Where are we going? What time should I be ready? How long will we be gone?"

"Wow, guess I ought let her out of the tower more often." Cal shook his head at his daughter.

Laughing, Gabby responded to her young friend. "It's a surprise, let's say nine, and plan to be gone the whole day."

With his daughter's mood greatly lifted, Cal relaxed visibly. *Thank you,* he mouthed when he was sure Minna wasn't looking.

The words were nice, but far better was the look in his eyes.

And what are you doing later tonight? she tried to communicate with her expression alone, unsure of how successful she was until Cal rose, ostensibly to buy dessert, and came back with a plastic-wrapped plate of cookies and a slab of apple pie that he set in front of her, along with a napkin and fork. Gabby was about to protest that she was too full to eat pie when she saw the note he'd written on the white napkin.

Meet me in the gazebo after the fireworks.

The Fourth of July lingered in the night sky, with firecrackers being detonated on residential streets long after the show in Doc Kingsley Park had concluded.

The scents of smoke and hot dogs, pickles and cotton candy would likely perfume the air until morning, but neither Cal nor Gabby noticed as they kissed in the darkness of the gazebo.

"No one wondered why you needed a babysitter at 10:00 p.m.?" Gabby asked between kisses, leaning into Cal's broad chest and the circle of his solid arms.

"Mmm…" he murmured, dropping kisses onto her forehead, her eyelids, her nose while his hands caressed her back. "I may have implied I was going to do my civic duty by cleaning the park."

"Irene Gould is on the Honeyford Days committee. She knows who volunteered." Gabby stretched up to nibble his full lower lip. "And cleanup is scheduled for tomorrow, which is why we're the only people left in the park. I bet she saw right through you."

Moving his hands lower, Cal pressed Gabby close so she could feel the effect her lip-nibbling had on the lower half of his body. "Do you care?" His deep growl sent vibrations ringing through her.

"Not enough."

They kissed until they were panting.

"Let's go," Cal said when they broke apart, taking her hand. Gabby didn't have to ask where they were going, though she was surprised he remembered the path to their oak tree after a decade and a half.

All these years later the tree still stood apart from its

fellows, in a clearing not far from the creek. Standing
guard over a flat patch of earth, the oak provided the perfect canopy for picnics and the type of monkey business
Cal had in mind.

"Are you positive this is the same place?" Gabby whispered, the excited pounding of her heart making a full
voice impossible.

"I'd know it in my sleep," Cal whispered back. "I've
seen it in my dreams."

He took her face in his hands and her mouth with his.

Gabby felt as if their bodies were melting into each
other, no separation to distinguish who was who as they
commemorated Independence Day, paradoxically, by becoming one, body and soul.

"Tell me everything—and I mean every single micro-
scopic detail no matter how insignificant you think it may
be—about you and Caleb Wells. Gee, I hope I don't sound
nosy."

Lesley swept into Gabby's house a half hour before the
start of dance class. With water bottle in hand ("Hydrate,
hydrate"), she planted herself on Gabby's sofa, pinning
her sister-in-law with a knowing stare.

"Every time I saw the two of you on the Fourth of
July—" she held up a hand "—not that I was looking—
you were sitting next to each other, standing next to each
other or undressing each other with your eyes. Gabrielle
Ann Coombs, has Cupid taken aim and shot you in the
hiney?"

Shutting the front door, Gabby followed Lesley to the
living room. "Les, I implore you, do not make too big a
deal about this. Cal and I are…exploring right now, that's
all. We're staying calm and rational and being highly cog-
nizant of the fact that he has a young daughter, and I have

a family and a new job. We're not going to rush into anything or make assumptions that would only confuse or hurt our family members in the end."

Gabby had rehearsed that little speech for the past few days, and she was pleased it had flowed rather effortlessly off her tongue. She gazed at Lesley with equanimity.

"Yeah, but have you done it?" her best friend demanded.

Sinking into a club chair, Gabby dropped her head to her hands, allowing a long groan before she peeked up at Lesley. "Did we really look like we were undressing each other with our eyes? Do you think anyone besides you noticed?"

"Nahhh. A couple people, maybe. Eric, for sure. Irene Gould. Claire." Lesley sucked water through a plastic straw. "And Claire might have mentioned something to Fletcher, I'm not sure." She waved a hand. "Don't worry about it."

Too agitated to remain seated, Gabby crossed to the bookshelf where she'd been packing into blue plastic bins the volumes she didn't plan to take on the ship. Grabbing an armful of hardcover novels, she wedged them in.

"Why are you still packing?" Lesley asked. She appeared both surprised and disappointed.

Gabby looked at her and sighed. "This is why I don't want to talk about Cal and me. Nothing has changed, Les. I'm still leaving."

Lesley smiled tenderly. "Gab, if you're in love, everything's changed."

Tears, those dratted, unexpected tears that popped up far too regularly now, tickled Gabby's nose. "I put my life on hold for years. For a man." She held up a hand to stay any comment Lesley might rightfully have made about her and Dean. "And I know that other time wasn't real.

But it *felt* real. I gave up growing and going on adventures and living my life because of a…a *feeling*. I can't do that again."

"Even if this time the man is feeling something in return?"

That was the question that had been keeping Gabby from achieving more than a few hours of sleep a night for the past several nights. In eight short weeks she would board a ship bound for the Hawaiian Islands, New Zealand and Australia. More importantly the ship and the wide oceans it sailed were a symbol of the large life she had always denied herself.

She *loved* being with Cal. And he seemed to love being with her. For now.

"I don't know how Cal feels."

"Ask."

"Even I know it's too soon for that."

Lesley balked. "Too soon? You've known each other since you were thirteen."

"And Cal has wanted to be part of my family since he was thirteen."

"Gab, what are you saying?"

Half-guilty, Gabby looked away. Family had always been a tremendous lure for Cal—her family, in particular, which had filled a void he hadn't been able to fill any other way. What if…just what if the relationship with her was more about his wanting to be part of a loving family than it was about his falling in love with her? That "what if" had the potential to break her heart.

Gabby knew that if she fell in love with Cal, really, truly, one-hundred percent in love, she might not be able to fall out of love with him the way she had with Dean. If she let him have her heart then discovered he was as much in love with the idea of family as he was with her, she just might accept that halfhearted love in lieu of the real thing.

She had settled for unrequited affection for the first half of her life. This time, she didn't want to settle for anything less than she was able to give.

Where Cal was concerned, she needed to protect herself…from her own burgeoning feelings.

"I've lived a small life, Les."

"There are plenty of people in this town who would see it differently."

Gabby smiled. "Thanks." What else could she say? Lesley had found the love of her life in Eric, who quietly worshipped the ground upon which his hilarious wife walked. She had two bright, humorous, adorable daughters. She'd found the path she was meant to walk early on.

"Listen, nothing personal, but I need to get ready for my ballroom class," Gabby said, giving her sister-in-law the bum's rush as delicately as she could. "My dance teacher hates it when her students are late."

"Yeah, yeah." Lesley rose. "You don't have to knock me over the head. I can mind my own business." Slinging a giant gym bag over her shoulder and sipping water along the way, she headed for the door. "Oh, by the way," she mentioned before she left, "tonight we'll be learning salsa, one of the sexiest ballroom dances. And since I like my salsa spicy, I'm eager to see whether you and Caleb can handle the heat."

"No way. We're getting haircuts?"

Minna stood outside Delilah's Hair Hive, her disappointment a nearly palpable thing as she discovered her big day out was going to take place in a beauty salon in Honeyford.

Gabby took no offense nor did she falter in her decision, sure that once Minna discovered what the day entailed she'd be as thrilled as any ten-year-old girl who was about to be treated like a woman.

Pulling open the glass door, she waited for Minna to enter.

"Are you sure kids are allowed in here?" Minna whispered.

"Absolutely," she reassured, sensing the girl's intimidation. "In fact, you might call this Kid Day at Delilah's."

They crossed the threshold into the silent salon.

"There's no one here," Minna observed.

"True. Delilah's is usually closed on Sundays."

Before Gabby could explain further, the salon's namesake clicked across the tile floor in spiky stilettos that would no doubt have sent Gabby crashing to the floor. Delilah appeared as hip and styled as she had the day she'd given Gabby her makeover.

"Well," the modelesque woman purred upon seeing her client, "you must be Minna. Short for Minerva, I presume? Minerva, Roman goddess of wisdom. I hope you're ready for a spa experience, Miss Minerva." She turned and *click-click-clicked* across the floor, obviously expecting Minna and Gabby to follow.

Gabby noticed Minna's gait become more labored as the girl battled increasing tension. "Don't worry," she whispered, walking beside her young friend, "Delilah knows what she's doing. You're in excellent hands."

"But you said she's closed on Sundays."

"I am," Delilah called back without turning around. "I only open for very special clients and friends on Sundays. We need music." She flipped a switch on a sound system perched atop a glass shelf that was bolted into the pumpkin-colored wall. The voice of Taylor Swift filled the salon. Gracing Minna with a brief smile, Delilah *click-*

click-clicked to her styling station. "Gabby is becoming a friend," she said, in her matter-of-fact way, devoid of sentimentality, "and you're a very special client. Have a seat." The back of the chair received a couple of quick pats that showed off Delilah's long nails.

Minna glanced around. "Um…where should I put my crutches?"

"Here." Delilah took the crutches and set them aside then stood patiently, making no move to help as Minna got herself into the chair. Once her client was settled, Delilah immediately got down to business, lifting sections of the girl's long dark hair.

"Are you going to cut it?" Worry edged Minna's words.

Leaning down, her well-coiffed head level with Minna's, Delilah smiled into the mirror, more warmly and more genuinely than Gabby had yet seen from the stylist.

"I'm not going to do anything you don't want me to do," Delilah assured. "Today is about you, Minna. Bringing out the qualities you most like in yourself. Showing the world how unique and wonderful you are. And from what I'm seeing so far, that won't be difficult at all. Shall we get started?"

Forty minutes later, Gabby stood excitedly in the salon's reception area, waiting for Delilah and Minna to emerge from the back, where they had disappeared after a shampoo, head massage, deep conditioning treatment and haircut. Minna's hair still required a blow dry and style, but first they had another surprise for the ten-year-old.

Gabby had purchased a dress in a gorgeous lilac shade to highlight Minna's dramatically contrasting dark hair and fair skin. She didn't believe that "clothes make the man" or woman, but she'd learned firsthand lately that they could make a girl feel more confident. She wanted Minna to have the whole makeover experience.

Delilah had offered to show Minna to the restroom and must have waited for her or helped her to change, because they were both gone a good fifteen minutes before returning to the front of the salon, Delilah offering an arm on which Minna could lean in lieu of her crutches.

"Oh, Minna, you look beautiful!" Gabby exclaimed, thrilled that the dress did, indeed, highlight her coloring. Even with her hair still damp, Minna looked lovely, though her shy smile suggested the transformation had not yet had the desired effect.

"She is beautiful, but we've only just begun," Delilah responded in Minna's stead. "Time to finish the hair then move on to the nails."

At this, Minna giggled, smiling broadly as if she could no more prevent the delighted stretch of her mouth than she could the sun from rising. A warm sense of satisfaction spread through Gabby's chest. So far, this had been a good idea. Perhaps Minna would respond positively to the next idea Gabby intended to present.

An hour later, Minna was staring into one of the salon's several large mirrors, beaming and occasionally laughing at her own reflection. "This is hot. This is so totally, totally hot."

"Glad you like it." Delilah tilted her head, considering her work. "Just remember, if you're 'hot,' it's because there's a fire burning inside you. No stylist can fan a flame that isn't there to begin with. And fire emanates from who we are far more than it does from the way we look."

Minna looked at her. "Yeah, but I'm the same person I was before you cut my hair, and I didn't look like this when I left the house."

"You did," Gabby interjected. "You just didn't know it yet." It was the same thing Cal had told her.

His daughter smiled and shrugged. *Whatever.* "I love

my hair. And this dress." She lifted the sheer overskirt, obviously wanting to twirl like any other girl in a swirly dress, and Gabby wished she could, just this once. "Thank you so much." Minna flashed white teeth and a perfect dimple. "Both of you!"

Delilah and Gabby accepted the thanks then shared a glance. Was it time to launch their attack?

"Let's do your nails now," Delilah said, nodding to Gabby.

"Mine?" That wasn't part of the plan.

"Nothing personal," Delilah said, "but your cuticles are a mess. You use your hands on the job, don't you?"

"Of course."

"Then you want your nails to reflect your professionalism and self-esteem."

"Oh. Okay."

Minna laughed, clapping her hands, delighted to have her new friend share in the beauty treatments. "Let me pick out your nail polish! Can I?"

When they were all seated and Delilah was busily filing Gabby's nails into neat ovals—"Forget trends, follow the natural shape"—Delilah mentioned as casually as if she were discussing the best hair product to provide lift at the roots, "I used to volunteer as a stylist for a pageant, did you know that, Minna?"

"A pageant? You mean a beauty pageant, like Miss America?"

"Beauty, talent, community service—the pageant I worked with honored all sorts of achievements. Primarily it was a chance for each contestant to choose the attributes she most enjoyed about herself, develop and share them with others. It's a pageant I think you might like to participate in."

Looking up sharply from where she was browsing The

Hair Hive's polish selection, Minna frowned. "You think *I* should be in a beauty pageant?"

Delilah arched a brow. "I told you, it's far more than a beauty pageant, and, yes, I think you'd do beautifully. In fact, I'm certain of it."

"I'm sure of it, too," Gabby said, grateful Delilah had broken the ice. "Which is why I'd like to sponsor you. What that means is Honey Comb's will provide anything you need to do the show. Clothes, props for the talent portion, transportation—that kind of thing." When she'd mentioned the pageant to Cal, he had been cautious, but willing to have Gabby present the idea to Minna. He'd insisted on taking care of any costs incurred if his daughter agreed to do the pageant, but Gabby greedily wanted that pleasure to herself.

"And I'd be happy to be your personal stylist," Delilah added, surprising Gabby as they hadn't discussed that possibility. She wondered whether someday Delilah would divulge more about her daughter.

Minna let the bottle she was holding clatter back to its spot on the tray of nail polishes. "I can't be in a pageant. That's, like, a really lame idea."

Though she'd anticipated the possibility of a moment like this, had even discussed it with Cal, Gabby tensed. Delilah squeezed her hand, which she understood immediately to be a warning not to overreact.

Continuing to work on Gabby's nails, not even bothering to glance up, Delilah asked, "Why?"

"Are you kidding? Have you seen me walk? Do you really think I want to look like a dork on a runway?"

"Well, if you think you'll look like a 'dork' on a runway, I can only assume you believe you look like a dork everywhere else you walk."

A gasp escaped Gabby's lips before she could stifle it.

Afraid Delilah had hurt Minna's feelings, her mind spun
with possible ways of undoing any damage. Apparently
understanding the direction of Gabby's thoughts, Delilah
gave her hand another firm squeeze. To Minna, she stated,
"You're not a mind reader or a prophet. You can't possibly
know what an audience full of human beings is going to
think. You don't even know what people on Main Street
are thinking. So I can only assume you're projecting your
opinion of yourself onto the people you see."

Whoa. That was really…good…but was that any way
to speak to a ten-year-old? A ten-year-old with a legiti-
mate disability?

Gabby made big eyes at Delilah, trying to tell her to
cool it a little, but the gorgeous brunette kept her gaze
lowered to her work.

"Well, now," Gabby stepped in, "I wouldn't say—"

"You mean *I* think I look like an idiot," Minna interrupted, focusing on Delilah, "and so that's how come I
think other people are thinking the same thing?"

Trading a file for a nail buffer, Delilah nodded.

Minna's face contorted in an uncharacteristic pout.
"How do you know? You're perfect. You probably never
have to worry about looking stupid."

Delilah's lips rose slightly, but with what Gabby per-
ceived as irony rather than humor. This time she did make
eye contact with Minna. "Maybe I try to look 'perfect' so
no one will see the truth."

"What's the truth?"

Setting down her manicure tools, Delilah stared calmly
but directly at Minna. "I can feel as broken on the inside
as you think you are on the outside. The more you guess
what other people are thinking, Minna, what their experience of life has been, the more chances you give yourself

to be wrong." She stood. "Come. I want to introduce you to someone who I think will be able to help me explain."

Balancing on her skyscraper heels, Delilah clicked across the floor.

Gabby stood, forcing herself to do no more than smile encouragingly as Minna decided whether to follow.

"There isn't anyone else here, is there?" Minna asked.

"Not in the flesh, no," Gabby responded, aware of where they were headed and admittedly curious about what else Delilah intended to say. Following Minna, she walked to the area of the salon where the poster of Delilah's daughter hung.

"'Miss You Can Do It,'" Minna read the words that curled across the bottom of the picture and graced the sash on the grinning girl in the photo. "That's the pageant you want me to do?"

"Mmm-hmm," Delilah confirmed, her own gaze magically softening as she looked at the poster.

"And that girl won it."

"It's not the kind of pageant you win or lose. She was one of the contestants, though, yes. What do you think of her? Just by looking, I mean. Can you tell me something about her?"

"She has a lot of friends."

"How do you know?"

"She's blonde and smiling and super pretty. And she looks really happy."

"Almost perfect?" Delilah asked.

Minna glanced at Gabby. *It's a trick question, isn't it?* Gabby shrugged back.

"I don't know," Minna said, hedging her bets, "I don't see anything wrong with her."

"You would have if you'd seen her in person."

"If I saw her walk you mean?" Minna asked, perking up.

"She didn't walk." Pulling her gaze from the poster, Delilah looked at Minna. "She rolled. Elyse used a wheelchair. She was in a car accident when she was two years old. It left her a paraplegic."

"What's that?"

"It means she could use her arms, but not her legs."

"Not at all?"

"No. She was fast, though." Delilah smiled. "She used to organize relay races down the halls in her school, even though she was the only one in a chair. I can't tell you how many calls I received from the principal, telling me he'd have to send Elyse home if she didn't stop racing."

"That girl, Elyse, is your daughter?" Minna's interest continued to grow.

Delilah hesitated only briefly. "That girl *was* my daughter. For nearly eleven years." She looked seriously at Minna. "Eleven extraordinary years. But not perfect ones."

Gabby's breath caught in her throat. For a moment, the salon was as silent as a church.

"What happened to her?" Minna asked.

"She had pneumonia. Most children can recover from it. She wasn't able to."

"I'm so sorry," Gabby said.

"That sucks," Minna said at the same time then slapped a hand over her mouth. "Oops. Sorry."

"Don't be." Delilah laughed. "It absolutely sucks."

Gabby shook her head. Delilah had obviously had a lot of practice at maintaining her composure. Though her brown eyes flashed with emotion, she remained poised, maintaining her connection with Minna.

"Would you like more information about the pageant?" she asked.

Minna's eyes moved from Delilah to the poster and back. It seemed to Gabby that a long time elapsed, but it was probably no more than seconds before Minna answered, "Yes."

Another hour later, their mani-pedis complete, all three women were playing with Delilah's makeup when Cal came to the door of the salon, looking more masculine than ever against the ultra-feminine backdrop.

Delilah let him in after she'd ushered Minna to the rear of the salon once more.

"You must be Cal. And you're here to pick up your dates, I presume?"

"That's right." As prearranged, Cal was escorting his daughter and Gabby to dinner. "And you're Delilah. Gabby's told me many good things. I appreciate what you're doing today."

"I'm a stylist. I'm just doing my job."

Delilah's demeanor around Cal was far different from her demeanor around Gabby and Minna. Still poised and confident, she was, nonetheless, a bit brittle. Cal seemed to sense her discomfort and pressed his gratitude only with a smile.

Gabby felt certain Delilah's attitude was not due to Cal, per se, but rather to his gender. Curiosity running rampant, Gabby wondered how Delilah had been able to snag—and keep—so many of Honey Comb's male clients. Then again, the sheer force of her sex appeal probably distracted most men from paying any attention to the subtleties in her attitude.

If Gabby were staying in town, maybe she'd work on her own sex appeal and attempt to get her AWOL clients to return. It might be fun to give Delilah a friendly run for her money.

Within a nanosecond, the thought of competing with Delilah on the basis of sex appeal made Gabby laugh out loud.

Cal grinned at her. "You seem mighty happy," he commented. He crossed the few steps that parted them and kissed her in an ostensibly friendly manner. In other words, ever so close to her mouth but not exactly on it, which made her want to grab him and plant a big one smack on his lips. "Hello, gorgeous," he murmured for her ears only.

Ohhhhhh, mama.

Dang, he looked yummy. And sounded yummy. She recalled the taste of his lips the night before. He was yummy.

While Gabby tried not to swoon in public, Cal glanced around the shop. "Where's my fabulous daughter? I can't wait to see what you've done." He hooked a brow in the salon owner's direction. "Gotta be honest, though. I think you're trying to improve on perfection."

Delilah, who seemed to be softening a bit, instructed, "If you'll wait here, we'll be right out." She disappeared down the hallway that led to the restroom and changing area.

The instant Delilah was out of sight, Cal slipped his arms around Gabby and pulled her close. "I'd kiss you properly, but I'm afraid the outcome would be highly improper." Instead, he lowered his head so that they were touching foreheads and noses. "How's your day been?"

It's so much more wonderful now that you're here.

"Pretty darn good," she answered. "Yours?"

"I missed you. The more we see each other, the more I miss you when we're apart." Humor resided in the crinkles around his eyes, but his voice dropped to a serious whisper. "I wonder what that means?"

A hundred panicky butterflies beat their wings in Gabby's stomach. "That you need more friends?" she cracked, a feebly humorous attempt to handle the emotions that started churning inside her.

Had the air-conditioning broken in The Hair Hive? Gabby was warm. Hot. Beginning to perspire.

"You know what they say about friends." She laughed. Lamely.

"What?"

"What?" *Oh, damn.* Of the hundreds of quotes filed in her brain (and there were at least a dozen regarding friendship) not a single one deigned to materialize. "Uh…"

Why was she so anxious? Nothing Cal had said or done implied anything stronger that what she'd been feeling.

Bingo.

She looked at him, at the face she had known for so long, still beautiful at thirty-three, his expressions interestingly softened by time and living, but their intensity undiluted. He'd taken all that hungry need of his youth and turned it into the motivation to become a good man. A great father. A compassionate lover.

Oh, criminy!

Gabby's heart seemed to lurch to a stop and remain that way a moment, allowing her a tiny break to evaluate the situation. Did she truly l-l-lo… Was she honestly in l-l-lo—

"Lady and gentleman," Delilah's throaty voice preceded her reappearance in the hallway.

Somehow—probably the startle reflex—Gabby had the presence of mind to step away from Cal (it was more like a leap) so that Minna would not see them plastered together. Her heart chugged into action again, and though

Cal moved far more slowly than she in removing his hand from her waist, they looked like a normal pair of friends (except for the fact that Gabby was bright red and hyper-ventilating) when Delilah headed toward them, support-ing a winsomely grinning Minna, sans crutches, on her arm.

"May I present Miss Minna Wells, shining star if ever there was one."

"Min." Sounding more like an exhalation than a spo-ken word, the whispered name brought Gabby back to her senses. Today was about Cal's daughter, the most impor-tant woman in his life.

"Min," he said again, obviously at a loss for words, and his reaction was so sweet Gabby was able to focus again on the world outside her. Her speeding heart and thoughts beginning to slow, she turned her attention to Minna.

Present for the entire day, Gabby hardly expected to be surprised when she saw the finished product. Delilah hadn't made huge changes to Minna's hair in any case, and she'd kept the makeup to a minimum. But the first glimpse of Minna, giggling and hopeful and so heart-breakingly happy, would make anyone's breath catch.

She was beautiful. A girl who would fill any mother's heart with enough pride to make it burst wide open. Not for the first time, Gabby wondered how Victoria could bear to live so far away. Even though she knew noth-ing of the other woman's feelings or her situation, Gabby couldn't fathom leaving a child like this to move halfway across the world.

A moment before she ran to get her camera, Gabby looked at Cal. The tears that filled her own eyes were re-flected in his. He was looking at his daughter, not at her, yet Gabby felt a connection to him like molten steel—hot, expansive and capable of turning into something that out-lasted either of them.

Oh, boy. There's trouble ahead.

In the past few months, Gabby had made a number of decisions about her life, wise decisions, brave decisions. The bravest she'd ever made.

Now she sensed she hadn't even begun to explore the courage it took to live a big life. Or the courage it took to consider that the biggest life of all might be right here in this room.

Chapter Thirteen

Three weeks passed with Gabby and Cal continuing their relationship as it was: Meeting for a "friendly" lunch most days of the week. Taking Minna swimming and trail riding and turning on the music in the living room one night after dinner so they could all practice the waltz. Gabby had come up with the idea that Minna would be able to "dance" if she stood on Cal's feet.

Because the movement of Minna's legs was occasionally unpredictable, Gabby had tied their shins together using scarves and told Minna to relax as completely as she could while Cal moved. The three of them had laughed like hyenas at first, but as they'd buckled down and gotten serious, it had worked! Cal and Minna had been able to dance again, with Cal negotiating the steps and Min reveling in the movement, like she had when she was small enough to perch in Cal's arms.

And, of course, there were the nights after Minna went to bed. Velvet, magical nights.

Lovemaking was turning out to be something Gabby enjoyed more than any other physical activity she'd ever tried. The sensation of living one hundred percent in the moment, of being awash in sensation, out of control herself and yet fully in charge of another person, was inexplicably wondrous. And always there was a moment of absolute perfection, when she felt wholly at peace in their mutual embrace.

Like puzzle pieces, Cal and Minna were fitting themselves into her life and into Honeyford. Only Gabby seemed unable to wedge herself firmly into place. Anyplace. Every day she found it more and more difficult to commit herself mentally either to her new job or to the thought of remaining in Honeyford.

"You can't make the pieces fit because you're not sure what the completed puzzle is supposed to look like," Lesley responded sagely when Gabby expressed her confusion about her future.

"That's so wise!" Gabby said, hungry for some relief from the turmoil raging inside her as she and Lesley race-walked for fitness. "I'm scheduled to get a physical for my new job," she said. "And I'm supposed to fly to Los Angeles in August for a five-day orientation. I was so excited when they first told me about it. The travel, the change from the norm—it's exactly what I wanted when I applied for the job. When I think about giving it up, I start to panic, literally panic."

"Have you spoken to Cal about this?"

"No. We tend to avoid the subject."

"Denial," Lesley panted as she strode along. "Not just a river in Egypt."

The late July afternoon was hot, and the women were sticky. Nonetheless, Lesley raised her elbows, picking up the pace of their walk. "I can't believe I'm saying this, because I think he's wonderful, but you need to stop seeing Cal for a while. Throw yourself into getting ready for the cruise. If you can handle it—I mean, if you're excited about leaving and not dying inside at the thought of leaving him—then…"

"Then what? Then what?" Gabby wheezed, struggling to keep up physically and otherwise.

"Then—and again, I cannot believe I'm saying this—but you'd better go. Live the life you say you've been avoiding all these years. Find out what you've been missing. You don't necessarily have to break up with Cal, anyway. You could do the long-distance thing."

"Hmm."

"Has Minna figured out yet that you're an item?"

"I'm not positive, but I think so." Gabby's lungs labored pathetically as they headed up one of Honeyford's few hills—Old Farm Road, leading to the farm belonging to Honeyford's original beekeepers. The closer they got, the more bees the women had to contend with on the dirt path. Lesley didn't mind, but Gabby was as tired of batting the critters away as she was of batting away her thoughts. Pulling her Ducks cap lower on her head as one especially pesky insect insisted on getting too close for comfort, she said, "Minna keeps giving us knowing looks and grinning or giggling when she leaves a room."

"Ah." Les nodded. "Bummer. Kids can be pretty black and white. Cal's going to have a tough time explaining that he's still in a relationship with you if you're nowhere to be found."

Like her mother.

Oh, this was miserable! Gabby felt as if her mind was laboring harder than her body. Falling in lo-lo-… Falling in lo-…

Dang it!

Realizing you finally wanted a relationship with someone was a monumental bummer when you were on the verge of starting your life someplace else. What she knew—absolutely—about Cal was that he wanted a family, the traditional family for which he'd waited his whole life. Traditional at least in the sense that they were all in the same city.

Minna deserved a mother who put notes in her school lunches and polished her friends' nails during sleepovers and attended parent-teacher conferences. Cal deserved a wife who understood his deep longing for stability and for all the trappings of hearth and home and who helped him achieve that. The cruise line had already explained that Gabby would be spending many of her holidays aboard ship from now on.

Between her awareness that Cal needed family and her very real fear that he wanted her, at least in part, because she came as a package deal with a family he already coveted…well…she, too, was feeling pretty black and white about their relationship. Either she stayed—with him, or she left—alone.

When the bee that persisted in following her tried to land on her nose, Gabby squealed and tried to outrun it for several steps.

"Let's go!" she begged Lesley. "This road is a minefield of bees. I know it's the best hill for our glutes," she said before her fitness-minded BFF could protest, "but it's not worth it."

Lesley stopped walking. "Gabby, have you ever been allergic to bees?"

"No."

"Ever been stung while hiking this hill before?"

"No."

"Ever heard of a stinger that couldn't be pulled out eventually?"

Gabby thrust her hands onto her hips. "What is your point?"

Green eyes narrowed. "My point is if nothing *horrible* has happened to you so far, and odds are nothing *irreparable* is going to happen in the future, then why are you so damn afraid of a little risk?"

"Les, in thirty-three years of living in Honeyford, with beekeepers all around me, I have never gotten stung. Not once. That's a good track record. I'd like to hang on to it."

Lesley shrugged. "Okay." Pulling the ubiquitous water bottle from the holder fastened around her slim hips, she popped the top up, took a slug then closed it with a slap of her palm. "Although if never getting stung is your idea of a life's goal then we look at life very differently."

"Huh?" And then Gabby got it.

She looked at her sister-in-law, feeling sheepish and vaguely ashamed. "We're not talking about bees anymore."

"Nope."

Heeding Lesley's advice, Gabby tried to stay away from Cal for a time so she could gain some perspective. She quickly discovered, however, that resisting a night with him was like fasting for a week then being alone in a room with a plate of warm chocolate chip cookies and trying not to inhale. She simply couldn't do it. Over and over she told herself she would take a few days to gain some clarity, and then she'd see him and lose control of her mouth the moment he said, "How about dinner at our place?"

Tonight was an excellent example. She'd promised herself—*promised*—that she would spend the evening sorting clothes and kitchenware so the house would be cleaned out and ready to rent even before she left to board the ship. The plan was to stay at her parents' place when she was on dry land, helping out on the farm. Between rent for the cottage, her salary from the cruise and the money she'd make from the sale of Honey Comb's, assuming the place sold, she'd be able to build a nice nest egg. It was a sensible plan. But did she sensibly heed it? Noooooo.

Cal said, "How about dinner," she said, "I'll bring dessert," and here she was, seated on his sofa, much too close for comfort while Minna sat ramrod straight in a chair before the fireplace with a violin tucked beneath her chin. A large, hand-lettered sign announcing, "Violin Recital at 7:00 P.M. Pacific Standard Time. Free Admission" sat propped against the brick mantel.

Cal's feet tapped to the lively beat as Minna's right hand danced the bow across the strings. She'd taken violin lessons in Chicago and enjoyed the fact that she could control her upper body well enough to play the demanding instrument. But, Cal confided, she had never been as dedicated as she'd become since Gabby's mom started teaching her to fiddle.

"Boil Down the Cabbage" was a porch-stomping ditty capable of eliciting perspiration in the player and an irresistible urge to move in the listener. When he could sit still no longer, Cal rose and reached for Gabby's hand.

Her family had jigged to Nancy's playing many times in Gabby's youth, though she and her brothers had mainly goofed around. She couldn't recall a time when Cal had joined in.

Now she was the one who attempted to demur and he insisted, hauling her to her feet, bringing her around the coffee table and moving with abandon.

It didn't take long to be swept away by the spirit of the evening. Minna bounced on her chair, grinning hugely as she played. Cal's enthusiasm was contagious the way a child's enthusiasm for his first glimpse of Disneyland is contagious.

He's dancing with his own family now, Gabby realized. *He finally feels that he's truly part of the fun.*

Unable to begrudge him a single moment of the pleasure he'd deserved for years, she let herself go, collapsing in giggles as much as she danced. When finally Minna's arms were too tired to play anymore, Gabby collapsed onto the couch.

Her body metamorphosed into a wet noodle, she panted, "Water. Give me water."

Appearing more energized after all the exercise, Cal laughed, providing the requested water and root beer floats for everybody.

"I have three weeks to perfect my fiddling before the pageant," Minna said, pressing her index finger over the top of the straw, raising it and letting the creamy root beer drip into her mouth. "And I'm trying to read the entire online encyclopedia so I'll know current events and history in case anyone asks, 'cause pageant girls are always supposed to know that stuff. Oh, and guess what?"

"What?" Cal and Gabby said in unison.

"Ava Grogan from my camp said she and Emily Leighton and Kelsey Thacker are going to come to the pageant in Eugene! They already asked their mothers. Isn't that cool? Oh, my Lord, I'm so nervous!"

"It is totally cool, and you'll be just fine, butterfly." Cal looked like a man who'd been given a million bucks, tax-free. His daughter felt better about herself already and was allowing friendships as a result.

Minna squealed, her excitement impossible to contain. "Can I take my root beer float upstairs so I can start studying the encyclopedia?"

"Would it do any good to say I'd like you to relax and take it easy tonight?"

Minna's expression answered his question more vividly than words. Cal laughed and hitched his thumb over his shoulder. "Head up. I'll bring the root beer."

"Thanks for the recital, sweetie pie," Gabby said. "My mother is in heaven teaching you, by the way. She's finally getting over the fact that none of her children was ever any good at the violin."

"Nancy is awesome," Minna stated. "She told me I can call her Nana since I only have a Grandma Joan, and she's in Chicago." Giving Gabby a quick, happy hug, she headed for the stairs.

When Cal returned from escorting his daughter to her room, he suggested that he and Gabby take their floats out to the front porch.

"Seriously?" she asked. "When there's an empty living room with no eyes to see us, you know…making out a little?"

The grin that claimed Cal's face was as loaded with lust as it was laughter. "That's exactly why we're going outside. I am incapable of making out 'a little' tonight. We need to be somewhere safe since there's a very alert girl upstairs."

"Ah. That seems like a perfectly reasonable reason."

He got close enough to whisper words into her neck, making every little hair stand up. "Frustrating, though."

Paying him back for the sexual teasing, she put a hand low on his jeans and s-l-o-w-l-y pushed him away. "Terribly frustrating."

Half growling, half grinning, he took her hand and led her into the summer evening.

They settled onto chairs that sat side-by-side, and Cal

put his feet up on the porch railing. "This is a perfect night."

Gabby sipped her root beer float. "I think it's a little muggy."

Reaching over to loop a tangle of red hair around his finger, Cal said, "I'm not talking about the weather, curly top." They traded smiles and sat quietly for a time, enjoying the crickets and the distant sound of exuberant kids squeezing the last bit of light from the day. After a while, Cal said, "I've been trying to pay your mom for the violin lessons, but she keeps refusing. Says it's all in the family."

Cal's expression was one of such peace, such satisfaction that anyone watching would assume, "Here is a man who has everything he wants."

Alarm bells rang deep inside Gabby. She tried to quell them. A part of her knew Cal cared about her, truly cared. But a more clamorous part would not allow her to relax.

Fear, that damned ulcerating fear that cared little for common sense or reality, began churning in her stomach. How ironic that the thought of escaping to the wide, unfamiliar ocean made her feel in control, whereas the thought of staying with the people and places she'd known all her life made her feel powerless.

"Minna's going to a sleepover at her new pal Ava's house on August eleventh. How about joining me for an outdoor concert in Bend that night?"

Wired as she was, Cal's question made her jump. "August eleventh?" she repeated stupidly.

"Yeah."

She would be in Los Angeles on August eleventh, learning all about life aboard ship. Cal knew she was leaving to start work in September (although they hadn't discussed it in over a month), but she hadn't yet mentioned the orientation, because…well…

Because she was a yellow-bellied, lily-livered, conflict-hating avoider, that's why.

"August eleventh…." Root beer and ice cream crept up her throat. "I can't that night. I'm going to be in, um, Los Angeles."

Feet propped on the railing, icy glass balanced on his stomach, Cal turned to look at her. "Los Angeles, California?"

"Yes. That's where the cruise line's business office is located. The cruise line I'm planning to work for."

Gabby cowardly spoke without looking at Cal, but she felt his gaze and saw from the corner of her eye that he nodded slowly.

"You're not scheduled to leave until September." Flat and even his voice asked a question even though he'd made a statement.

"My job begins in September, that's right. I have to report to Los Angeles for an orientation first, though. The orientation lasts a week. I'll be back in time for Miss You Can Do It." At least she was ending on an up note.

When Cal said nothing, she knew she had to look at him.

He was staring at the street, at houses bathed in lavender twilight, their interior lights beginning to click on in living rooms and upper-floor windows. Another simple evening in Honeyford.

Having no idea what Cal was thinking, Gabby spoke the first thing on her mind.

"We knew all summer that we were heading toward this moment—when I would have to leave," she reminded him softly. "Didn't we? We should have been talking about it more. I've known I needed to bring it up again, but every

time I thought about it, we were having such a good time…
I never wanted to ruin the moment."

Setting his glass on the round table between their
chairs, Cal rose. He crossed to the far end of the small
porch, put his hands on his hips and stood silently a moment before turning to look at her. "It seems to me that
leaving town—even for a week—is something lovers discuss with each other. Assuming they're doing more than
having a summer affair."

Another statement embedded with a question. Gabby
wanted desperately to say what she had to say without
hurting him unduly. "It *is* more than an affair if two people care about each other. If they're going to go on caring
for each other even when…when they're not seeing each
other regularly, then it's definitely more than an affair."

"Bull."

Cal did not swear casually in public, and even though
no one was outside on his street, the vehemently spoken
word jarred Gabby.

"It's an affair if it's time-limited from the outset," he
said. "It's an affair if feelings don't figure into decisions
about the future."

He watched her as if he were looking for signs of life,
his intense eyes as focused as an eagle's.

Say it, Gabby. Just say it. She begged herself to get it
over with, to admit that she was going to leave no matter
what. That nothing he could do or say would change her
mind, because in the end she didn't want to feel all the
wild uncontrollable feelings she had for him, or the fears
that plagued her when she thought about staying.

Perhaps all she needed was a break from Honeyford. A
chance to prove to herself that she had the capacity to be
courageous and bold and to live without the man whose

every touch had, terrifyingly, begun to seem as essential as oxygen.

"My leaving isn't about us. It's about me, Cal. It's about something I need to do. I made the decision before you came back." She intended to rise, but her legs were shaking so badly she settled for scooting to the edge of her chair. "Maybe it won't be a permanent move. I don't know. I don't expect you not to move ahead with your life. But if I don't follow through with my plans, I'm afraid I'll always question myself. And that alone would ruin us in the end."

His gaze remained steady and searching through every word she spoke. Then he glanced away. A tiny, ironic smile tinged his lips. When he looked back, his face was a mask of acceptance.

"'Love and music—it's all in the timing.'"

"Who said that?"

"No idea." He watched her sadly. "But it seems to apply to us. Maybe someday we'll get the timing right."

They didn't hug goodbye. They certainly didn't kiss. Gabby asked if she could take Minna to Honey Bea's after camp the following day. Minna already knew Gabby was leaving to start her job in September, but Gabby wanted to tell her about L.A. and to assure the girl she'd be back in time for Miss You Can Do It.

And that was that.

No sustained drama. No aching goodbye. Not even a fight to make them both temporarily glad they didn't have to look at each other.

Gabby returned to her cottage and to her packing and to her pre-Cal-and-Minna plans. She told herself she had chosen the only course she could. She couldn't stay, filled with worries and fears and regrets. That couldn't possibly be the right thing to do.

No matter how she assured herself, though, she felt as if she'd just closed the most fantastic fireworks display ever by lighting a single sparkler. A great show deserved a fitting finale, yet she and Cal had sputtered halfheartedly to a close.

Chapter Fourteen

"Minna! Min! Are you done with breakfast?" Cal called into the kitchen from the living room. Now that he was working again, his office officially opened, getting Minna fed, suited up and to camp on time was a daily juggling act. When there was no response from the kitchen, he felt his irritation spike.

Gabby had been in Los Angeles four days. Since their conversation on his porch, Cal couldn't stand to pass by Honey Comb's or to glance at the gazebo in Doc Kingsley Park. The slightest problem annoyed him. He had to bite his tongue a hundred times a day.

He hadn't only asked her to a concert on August eleventh; he'd planned to ask her to marry him.

Rubbing his chest, where he seemed to have permanent heartburn lately, Cal silently called himself a few choice names. He had honestly believed he could seduce Gabby into realizing they belonged together. He had minimized her desire to leave town, he had lied to himself and he had ignored her needs every step of the way.

The result was pain all around.

Thankfully, Minna appeared to accept Gabby's decision. After a few tears, she had reassured herself and Cal that at least Gabby would be back in time for the pageant. So far, Cal had not discussed with his daughter what would happen in September, when Gabby's absence became more permanent. He figured they'd cross that narrow bridge when they came to it.

"Min!" He called out again, about to head to the kitchen when he heard a tap on the window.

"Out here, Dad." The sound was muffled, but he clearly saw his daughter, sitting on the porch. She smiled and waved him outside.

Opening the front door, he peered out. Minna was ready for camp, her backpack near her feet. "Hey," he said, surprised. "Did you eat breakfast?"

She pointed to the empty cereal bowl on the table.

"What are you doing now?" he asked, noting the drawing pad on her lap. "You need to brush your teeth."

"I will. I just want to finish this."

"Min, it's almost time to leave. If that's something else for the pageant—"

"It's not. I'm making a card for Gabby. Look."

Minna turned the sketchbook toward her father, and Cal read the large letters that filled the page. "'You can do it. We believe in you.'" Walking over, he took the pad and studied it. "What does this mean?"

"It means we're thinking of her. I figure if we're this sad that she's gone, then she must be really sad to be away from us, too. She probably needs some encouragement."

"I thought you were doing okay with it, butterfly."

"I am. But I'm still sad, and I don't want to be."

Cal sat down on the chair beside Min's, the same one he'd sat in when Gabby told him she was definitely leaving. He cleared his throat. "Min. It's okay to be sad. You know that, right? When people disappoint us—"

"I know it's okay, Dad. Sheez, you've told me it's okay to feel my feelings since I was probably, like, two."

"Actually, I started telling you when you were, like, one." He ruffled her hair, and she smiled.

"Anyway, Gabby didn't disappoint me, not really. She's only doing what she told me to do."

"What is that?"

Minna took the sketchpad back from her father and began coloring in the stars she'd scattered across the page. "Well, when I told her I was scared to do Miss You Can Do It, she said I didn't have to prove anything to the audience, but that I should show myself what I'm capable of. That I have a personal responsibility to shine my light. Do you know Gabby's hardly ever been anyplace but Honeyford, Daddy? She told me she's never even been to Chicago or ridden the el train. That's kind of sad, isn't it?"

Cal smoothed the hair he'd ruffled behind Minna's ear. "Yeah. I guess it is."

Looking up again, Minna gazed at her father with compassion far beyond her years. "I know you liked Gabby a lot, Daddy. A real whole lot."

Coming from the little girl he was forever trying to protect, the comment kicked him in the gut. Cal considered refuting the awareness he saw in her eyes, but it would do no good. So he just nodded. "Yep. A real whole lot."

Minna nodded back. She returned her attention to coloring the stars. "You know how when Mom left, you told me she wasn't leaving me, she was just leaving?"

"Yes."

"Well, I don't think Gabby's leaving us. She just needs

to shine her light, Dad. And we love her so we have to let her."

The heartburn in Cal's chest turned into a knot that clogged his throat. Tears burned his eyes.

He sat, watching Minna quietly, waiting for the tears to subside a bit so that he could tell his daughter how damn proud she made him. And how much he loved her.

The August morning began to heat up. The camp bus would rumble onto Main and Fifth in a short while. But for now, Cal didn't want to rush. He didn't want them to be anywhere other than exactly where they were.

And he saw no point at all in correcting his perceptive daughter's assertion that they both loved Gabby Coombs.

The following week, Caleb entered the house, wrung out from the past several days and grateful that Irene Gould was able to pick Minna up from the bus stop and spend afternoons with her now that he was working full-time. Occasionally, Irene and Minna even put dinner in the oven, which, he had to admit, he hoped they'd been able to do tonight.

Unfortunately, as he stepped into the foyer and removed his work boots, he acknowledged that he didn't smell a thing. Didn't hear anything, either.

"Hello! I'm home." He listened for the sound of Minna working on her computer upstairs. Nothing.

Maybe they were out back or gardening over at Irene's. If that were the case, he'd have time for a quick shower before he paid Irene and whisked his daughter out to eat. Heading for the stairs, Cal took the steps two at a time until he realized they were dotted with clothing. Girl clothing. He saw a pair of flip-flops…a T-shirt…jeans…

Fatigue made him grumble. "Min." He'd told his daughter a hundred times not to drop her clothing over the balustrade, that if she wanted to do her laundry, he'd carry the basket down for her. This habit of hers only made extra work.

Shaking his head, he retrieved the items as he climbed the stairs, trying to come up with a logical consequence for disregarding what he'd—

He stopped thinking when he picked up a scrap of pale pink fabric that looked like…a bra.

Holding it up, Cal turned the item this way and that.

It was a bra. Definitely not his daughter's.

"Irene?" he called warily, then shook his head. *Nah.*

There were more clothes and accessories up ahead. Cal followed the trail—a belt, tank top, a necklace—all the way to his bedroom.

His heart began pounding as he stooped to pick up the socks. By the time he put his hand on the knob of his closed door—which he was positive he'd left open this morning—his pulse was racing like a sprinter.

Turning the knob, he opened the door to the sweetest sight he could imagine…. Gabby—beautiful, seductive, hopeful and, unless he was mistaken, naked—looking at him from under the sheets in the middle of his king-size bed.

"It took a while," she said, her voice strong and tender and aching, "but I finally figured out that loving you is the biggest adventure of my life." She shook her head, huge gray eyes full of regret. "I've been a dunce."

Cal stepped into the room. "You're back."

She nodded. "Los Angeles didn't work out. I thought it was so brave of me to leave, but once I was away from you, I felt terrible. I knew nothing was ever going to be as exciting as being with you and Minna. So I decided to come back and admit that I lied about why I left in the first place."

At the moment, Cal wasn't sure he cared that she'd lied when she left or that she wanted to tell the truth now. She was back, and he wanted to grab her in his arms and shout hallelujahs to the rafters.

"Where are Minna and Irene?" he asked hoarsely.

"I sent them to the movies and dinner. Hope you don't mind. I figured that after the way I left I needed to make a showy return. You know, to get you to forgive me and give us a third chance."

Cal kicked the door shut with his heel.

"You are going to give me another chance, aren't you?" Gabby asked. "To get the timing right?"

"Timing?"

"The timing between us."

Cal approached the bed. When he got there, he dropped the bundle of clothes in his hands. "It's been a long damn week. If I'm only dreaming that you're here, I'm going to be mighty p.o'd."

Gabby smiled, but she clutched the sheet in front of her. "Cal, before you take another step, I need to tell you why I *really* left."

"Talk quick."

"Oh. Well, all right." She plucked at the sheet, obviously uncomfortable now that she had his full attention. His curiosity was piqued. "Well," she said again. "You see, once we were together awhile, I realized I lo—lo—" She stopped. Swallowed. Shook her head. Smiled. "I realized I l-l-lo— Oh, for crying out loud." She compressed her lips in disgust then shouted, "I love you! In a crazy, scary, uncontrollable way. And I was afraid that someday I might find out you didn't love me as much as I love you, and that if that were the case, I wouldn't be able to stand it."

"You had me at I love you," he said. "Gabby, you were

afraid I didn't love you enough? That's the damned dumbest thing I've ever—"

"Please. I'm not finished." She held up a hand. "See, I thought it might be better to stand on my own until I figured out how not to crumble. I know that sounds cowardly, but it's what I felt. And then it occurred to me." She slapped the heel of her hand against her head. "Gabby! You can't control how much you're loved. You can only control how much love you're willing to give. And that's when I decided to come back here and give you all the love I have. You and Minna. Because, Cal, nothing will ever, ever feel as exciting to me as an ordinary day with you."

Cal just looked at her. His Gabby. The first woman he'd ever loved. The only woman he would ever need. The woman he'd waited most of his life to love as openly and fully and completely as he wanted. His heart was so damn full he could hardly speak.

"What do you think?" she prompted, biting her lip.

What did he think?

"Are you wearing underwear?"

"Beg your pardon?"

"There were no panties on the stairs."

"Oh. A lingerie man. Come see for yourself."

"I'm going to. And I hope you sent Irene and Min to a double feature, because when I start showing you how much I love you, I'm not going to stop. For. A. Very. Long. Time."

"I think we have until nine," Gabby told him, smiling as he began removing his own clothing.

"Gabby," he said.

"Yes?"

"Until nine won't be long enough. In order to show you how much I love you, I'm going to need, at the very least, the rest of our lives." He tossed his shirt into the corner. "You have that much time?"

The sigh she released was rich with relief. "I do," she said. "I'm quite certain, Caleb Wells, that this time I can promise you a lifetime."

Cal hesitated. "I want to propose properly."

"That's fine, Cal. I'm looking forward to it. But could you do it later, please?"

Cal couldn't reach the bed—and his woman—fast enough.

Epilogue

Against a black backdrop that ran the length of the stage in Oregon State University's main theater, silver lights spelled out MISS YOU CAN DO IT, making the pageant title resemble a shooting star in the night sky.

The contestants glowed more brightly than the set.

Minna stood center stage with girls on either side of her, awesome girls she'd become friends with during the past few days of pageant activities. Every single one of them had something really unique about her, like Minna did. "Unique"—that was the word Delilah had told her to use instead of "weird" or "wrong."

Delilah had done Minna's hair and helped a bunch of the other girls backstage, too, and was now watching the pageant from the audience, with Cal and Gabby.

Minna blinked, trying to make her eyes adjust to the stage lights and the flashbulbs so that she could find a friendly face in the crowd.

She found twelve of them.

Surrounding Dad and Gabby, who sat third row center and had, for the past hour, been smiling the goofiest smiles Minna had ever seen in her life, there were more Coombses—Nancy and Frank, whom Minna called Nana and Papa; Uncle Ben, who wasn't really her uncle yet, but had gone around telling everyone his "niece" was in the Miss You Can Do It pageant and who had brought her the biggest, most embarrassing bouquet of flowers she'd ever seen; Uncle Dylan and Aunt Julie—same situation, not exactly relatives yet, but they'd already asked her to be a flower girl at their wedding, along with Minna's new cousins, Kate and Natalie. Kate and Natalie were sitting next to Uncle Eric and Aunt Lesley, who kept passing tissues to Gabby. Gabby had been crying a lot this week. Dad said it was because she was happy.

That's the way her new family was. They laughed like crazy, cried some and teased each other all the time. Minna was getting used to it. She *had* to get used it; next month her dad and Gabby were getting married, and she'd be a Coombs-Wells forever. That's what they told her, anyway: This family is forever. Minna even got to go on their honeymoon! Well, the second one. Dad was going to take Gabby on two. The second was a surprise; Gabby didn't even know about it yet. They were going to Australia so she wouldn't be sorry she turned down the cruise ship job to be a barber…and mom…in Honeyford.

Gabby was going to be her mom! They were already supergreat friends, but having her as a stepmom was going to be even better. Gabby figured she'd be a "wicked good" stepmother; Minna's father laughed pretty much every time she said that.

Minna had asked if she could be a flower girl at the wedding, but her dad said Gabby wasn't marrying just him; she was marrying them both, so it would be better if all three of them stood together in the church.

"And now—" the evening's host took the microphone, redirecting Minna's attention to what was happening on stage "—we would like to invite each of the young ladies to share a few words with the audience."

As the emcee made the announcement, some of the other girls giggled nervously. Speaking in front of a whole theater could make a kid anxious. Not Minna, though— not tonight. She knew exactly what she wanted to say.

Gabby said her grandpa Max had taught her there was a lot to be learned from other people, so Minna had started reading biographies in her spare time, which, she supposed, was one more weird...uh, unique...thing about her.

When it was her turn to speak, she raised her chin high, like Delilah had taught her to do.

"Before I came here," she said strongly and clearly into the microphone, "my dad gave me a book about a woman who was really different from other people. Her name was Helen Keller, and she said this very cool thing about her friends, about how they were part of the story of her life and that they made her feel a whole lot better about being who she was. They helped her realize that even though she couldn't see or hear or talk like some of us, she still had about a gazillion gifts she could share." Minna shrugged at the audience. "I'm like that, too. I'm not very good at walking, and I used to get pretty upset about it. But now I have friends who help me figure out all the things I am good at. It's pretty cool. They're pretty cool. Plus my dad says challenges are just barbells for the soul." She giggled. "He's sort of into quotes nowadays. Anyway, that's it." She nodded. "Thanks."

As applause scattered throughout the house, Minna stepped back, looking for the row of people with the biggest, goofiest monster grins—and the one woman with the tissue smashed against her nose. When she found them, she waved, smiling back with what was very likely a big, goofy monster grin of her own.

The story of her life. So far it was pretty fantastic.

* * * * *

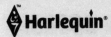
Harlequin®

COMING NEXT MONTH

Available September 27, 2011

SPECIAL EDITION

*Harlequin Romantic Suspense presents the latest book
in the scorching new* KELLEY LEGACY *miniseries
from best-loved veteran series author Carla Cassidy*

*Scandal is the name of the game as the Kelley family fights
to preserve their legacy, their hearts...and their lives.*

Read on for an excerpt from the fourth title
RANCHER UNDER COVER

*Available October 2011
from Harlequin Romantic Suspense*

"**W**ould you like a drink?" Caitlin asked as she walked
to the minibar in the corner of the room. She felt as if she
needed to chug a beer or two for courage.

"No, thanks. I'm not much of a drinking man," he
replied.

She raised an eyebrow and looked at him curiously as she
poured herself a glass of wine. "A ranch hand who doesn't
enjoy a drink? I think maybe that's a first."

He smiled easily. "There was a six-month period in my
life when I drank too much. I pulled myself out of the bottom of a bottle a little over seven years ago and I've never
looked back."

"That's admirable, to know you have a problem and then
fix it."

Those broad shoulders of his moved up and down in
an easy shrug. "I don't know how admirable it was, all I
knew at the time was that I had a choice to make between
living and dying and I decided living was definitely more
appealing."

She wanted to ask him what had happened preceding
that six-month period that had plunged him into the bottom

of the bottle, but she didn't want to know too much about him. Personal information might produce a false sense of intimacy that she didn't need, didn't want in her life.

"Please, sit down," she said, and gestured him to the table. She had never felt so on edge, so awkward in her life.

"After you," he replied.

She was aware of his gaze intensely focused on her as she rounded the table and sat in the chair, and she wanted to tell him to stop looking at her as if she were a delectable dessert he intended to savor later.

Watch Caitlin and Rhett's sensual saga unfold amidst the shocking, ripped-from-the-headlines drama of the Kelley Legacy miniseries in

RANCHER UNDER COVER

Available October 2011 only from Harlequin Romantic Suspense, wherever books are sold.

SPECIAL EDITION

Life, Love and Family

Look for
NEW YORK TIMES AND *USA TODAY*
BESTSELLING AUTHOR

KATHLEEN EAGLE

in October!

Recently released and wounded war vet
Cal Cougar is determined to start his recovery—
inside and out. There's no better place than the
Double D Ranch to begin the journey.
Cal discovers firsthand how extraordinary the
ranch really is when he meets a struggling single
mom and her very special child.

ONE BRAVE COWBOY,
available September 27 wherever books are sold!

Harlequin SHOWCASE 2 GREAT NOVELS 1 GREAT PRICE

USA TODAY Bestselling Author

RaeAnne Thayne

**On the sun-swept sands of
Cannon Beach, Oregon, two couples
with guarded hearts search for
a second chance at love.**

Discover two classic stories of love and family
from the Women of Brambleberry House miniseries
in one incredible volume.

BRAMBLEBERRY SHORES

Available September 27, 2011.

www.Harlequin.com

HSC68836